Orlo AND *Leini*

Orlo AND *Leini*

STORIES BY

RAFAEL ALVAREZ

Printed and bound in the United States of America.

1 2 3 4 5 09 08 07 06 05 04 03 02 01 00

Library of Congress Cataloging-in-Publication Data

Alvarez, Rafael, 1958-
Orlo and Leini / Rafael Alvarez.
p. cm.
ISBN 1-891521-07-1 (alk. paper)
1. Baltimore (Md.)--Fiction. I. Title.

PS3551.L848 O752000
813'.54--dc21

99-087708

Woodholme House Publishers
131 Village Square I
Village of Cross Keys
Baltimore, Maryland 21210
Fax: (410) 532-9741
Orders: 1-800-488-0051
Email: info@woodholmehouse.com

Book and cover design: Jason Lawrence and Lance Simons
Backcover photograph, author photo on page 176, and stories 3, 6: Jim Burger
Title page photograph and stories 1, 2, 4, 5: Elizabeth Malby
Cover illustration: Jonathon Scott Fuqua

for

A

ORPHEUM
cinema
ORLO AND LEINI

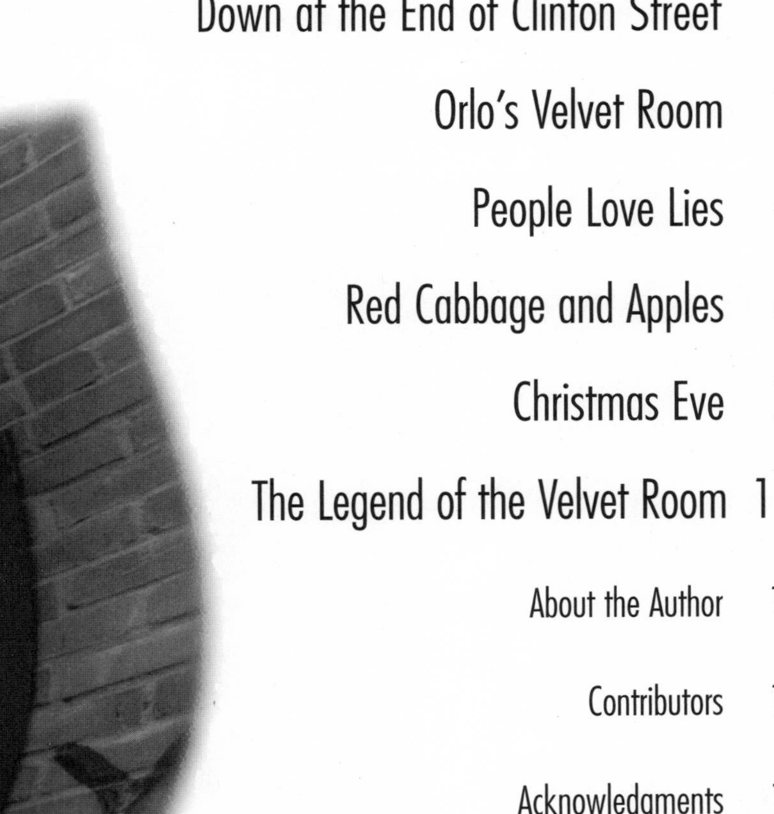

Orlo AND *Leini*

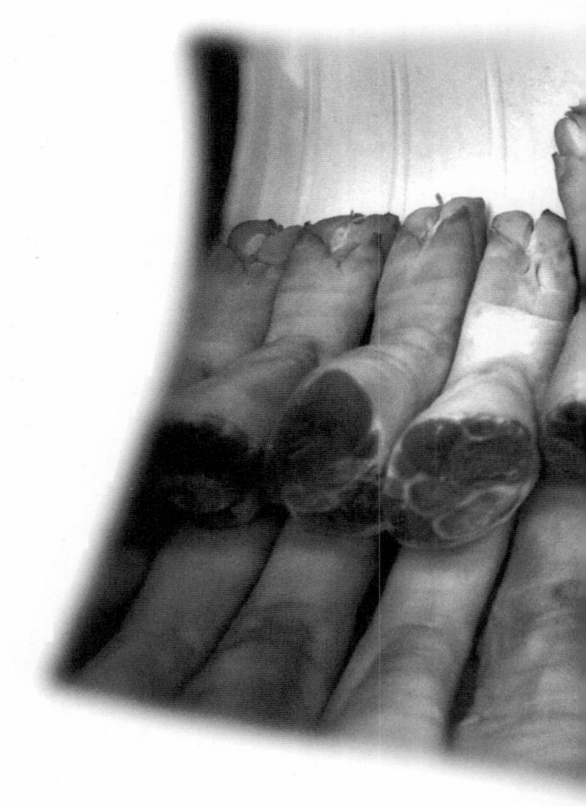

Insane, clandestine love . . .

Down at the End of Clinton Street

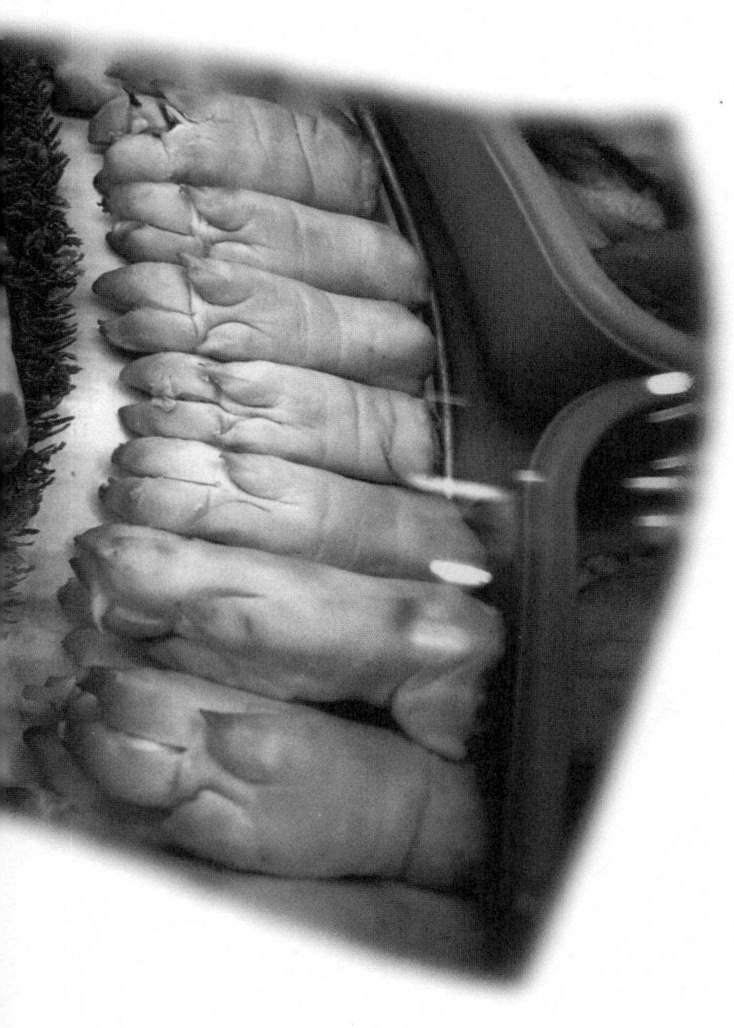

A half-century after he found love nibbling pig knuckles down at the end of Clinton Street, Orlo Pound's ashes lay in a candy tin the scavenger had rescued from the mud room of a Holy Land rowhouse.

Leini sat in the front row of mourners, eyes fixed on the Baltimore Clipper hammered into the tin, a rake cutting the sea.

In the requested moment of silence—moments for which no one prepares you; a kind word worth one gold coin and silence worth two—Leini remembered recipes stretching across half-the-century and Orlo thought of her.

The first five-dollar gold piece the junkman found on the sidewalk he could not tell you. And he forgot every tacky vase hauled out of some biddy's parlor the moment he turned it over.

But to this day, a pile of ashes in a can made for caramel creams, Orlo remembered every mote of dust that passed through the fading sunlight at Ralph's Lunch the first time he saw Eleini Leftafkis with her nose in a book.

No matter that it took fifty-two years—from Coolidge to Carter—for Leini to be seen with the junkman in any way that could not be construed as coincidental.

She was sixty-nine now; her daughter at her side in a metal folding chair in the mourning room of the Salvage House; deformed and unmarried and up against thirty, the same age as Orlo when the junkman asked Leini for a second helping of pig's feet at Ralph's Lunch.

Presiding at the service was a Unitarian circuit rider named Shane who lusted for the cathedral radios that Orlo collected; who years ago, upon receipt of a particularly fine wireless, had pretended to marry the lovers in a stand of peach trees behind the Salvage House.

It's only dress-ups, Leini told the preacher.

Make believe, said Orlo.

Shane, a brilliant thinker with more humor than faith, knew that Orlo and Leini were more married in their hearts than most who'd said "I do" in church.

"If there is a royalty among herbs, Eleini reigns sovereign," he eulogized. "No other is so revered for its beauty, fragrance, symbol, and use...in Spain it is the pilgrim blossom and children believe that the fairy babies sleep in its flowers. Where Eleini flourishes, the woman rules..."

Orlo knew he would love Leini through the end of this world and the one to come. It was one of the privileges afforded by death: No doubt.

He knew it the way scientists were certain—*almost certain*—that memory involves chemical changes in the nerve cells of the brain.

The way nothing—*almost nothing*—triggers memory more strongly than the scent of food wafting through an open window.

From pig's feet to porridge, there are tens of thousands of fragrances in this world and no two people receive them exactly the same way.

How does memory solidify?

The way pig's feet jellies in a pickling tub.

And the discarded cuts—feet and jowls, head, ears and tail; desired by the discerning and a plenty for the poor—sit on top of spaghetti.

All covered with cheese.

Love.

How do we form the memories that accompany us to the grave?

Through the marriage of repetition and intense emotion.

"Please stand," said Shane, walking the urn over to Leini—Orlo's lone bearer of pall—and leading the mourners out beneath the nickel sky for a funeral parade down a pier jutting out from the Salvage House to the harbor.

Little Leini walked alongside her mother, close enough for the old woman to lean if necessary. Balls Maggio pushed a bicycle hung with the crab nets he used to fish Pinkies out of the drink. The eighteen-year-old Basilio Boullosa, sad and stoned behind perfectly round shades, had cut art class at Transfiguration High to come, picking up his girlfriend Trudy on the way, blowing a quick joint with her in Orlo's peach orchard and talking about the recent, immeasurable loss of Keith Moon, wondering where, now that Orlo was gone, he would find the immense frames for his rock and roll landscapes.

(You will make them yourself, thought Orlo.)

Mr. Diz arrived with a fist full of Smiley Face balloons. Jimmy Jackson, the huge-hearted sport who gave Orlo tickets to ballgames for each lacrosse stick the junkman found and restrung, carried Novenas for an agnostic, all fourteen of his children in tow. William Donald Schaefer—utterly alone—paid respects to an old friendship based on a single question.

"How can we keep good people from leaving the city?"

Pio Talle traveled from his jewelry store at Eastern and Bouldin to thank Orlo for heirlooms discarded by thoughtless heirs. Bonnie Sabotka hauled a pocketbook full of Vidalia onions from the kitchen of her Elvis Bar. Virginia Baker—scolding Basilio that "that goddamn dope is gonna get you"—lumbered along with a box of jumping frogs and fliers advertising a square dance on the roof of the Broadway Recreation Pier.

At the last minute, *The Sun* dispatched Jay Spry from the rewrite desk to fetch six paragraphs, a few quotes, and a picture of the dead, but the story got held when eleven flakes of snow fell on Calvert Street.

The *News American* was as dead as Orlo, which is to say that it will never be forgotten, prompting "See Eddie" Lichtenberg to pass out "Orlo Lives!" t-shirts screened the night before in the basement of Shocket's, his South Broadway variety store.

Dantini the Magnificent declined to perform; it would be disrespectful, he said, in the face of the junkman's disappearing act captured for the ages by David Klein, a ship's carpenter who burned off rolls of black and white film with a camera that only worked in Baltimore and only then on certain streets.

H. Jefferson Knapp came as Honest Abe, a case of Scotch liberated from the High Step on his shoulder for the reception. Miss Fronie Lukowski took a day off from her floor scrubbing to say goodbye. Tom Nugent led a handful of hand-picked students from the College on the Hill to taste the essence of story.

Even Ted the Clown showed his orange and white face among scores of people from whom he'd bummed drinks, talking about the gold he'd sent Orlo's way as he strolled to the foot of Clinton Street with a Polish-Catholic girl who not only looked like Anne Frank's twin, but was just as smart and told the clown exactly where he could get off.

Good-hearted souls who knew of Orlo and Leini's great secret and never said a word; the people the junkman met in his travels—"I got my feelers out for you..."—and those who traveled to meet him.

Characters without end, for this is Baltimore.

All across the Holy Land, the Great Bolewicki Depression Clock tolled in harmony with the truth: "It's not too late for someone to pick up where Orlo left off..."

At the pier's end, Shane said a few more words he wasn't sure he believed and Leini moved to the edge, a brisk wind blowing the hem of the same black dress she'd worn for years: heavy veins pulsing beneath black knit stockings rolled to the crease of purple knees.

Leini shook Orlo's ashes into the cold Patapsco, licked her thumb and traced it around the crevices of the tin. Licking her thumb again, she passed the tin to Little Leini and took a large navel orange from the folds of her dress, peeling it as though there were all the time in the world.

(There is.)

Holding a piece of rind close to her face, Leini squeezed it to see the spray, a bit of magic unknown to Dantini that Orlo had shown her one difficult day to give her something real.

"Never explain your tricks," he'd told her, licking her tears. "No matter how clever, explanation always disappoints."

Leini tossed the rind into the harbor and followed it with her Class of 1926 ring from Patterson Park High School, a Baltimore Clipper coursing through the blue stone.

And then she slipped a piece of the orange into her mouth and turned for home, the crowd parting to let her pass. As the wind swept Orlo's ashes across the water, an ancient oiler from the engine rooms of Oslo named Mr. Olie took a belt from a flask and yodeled to Orlo's ghost.

"I like-a you, you like-a me...?"

They met on Goose Hill, three-and-a-half miles east of Monkey Row and as far south of Patterson Park as you can go without getting wet.

Ralph's Lunch on one side of Clinton Street.

Orlo's Salvage House on the other.

On a humid Feast of the Holy Cross in September of 1926—a summer after Leini had graduated third in her class behind the son of a Jewish grocer and the daughter of a German one—Orlo stopped at Ralph's for some food and the glass of beer that marked the end of his daily wanderings.

He threw a tarp over the day's haul, a small breeze drying the sweat on his neck, just before he would speak, at last, to the girl about whom he'd heard so much; more, finally, than a glimpse of her arms sunk in dish water or the wisp of a skirt turning a corner.

It was Leini's birthday and she sat on a stool against the wall near the kitchen; following a gang of Americans not much older than herself as they drank and lied their way through Paris and Spain; waiting for Mrs. Ralph or her husband to give her something to do when all they wanted was to have her close and know she was safe, keeping the promises they'd made to her family back in Greece.

Leini's book was new, borrowed that day from the Goose Hill branch of the Enoch Pratt Free Library up the street; its spine bending for the first time as Leini waited for something to happen in an American life where the local library, Ralph's lunchroom, and the Greek Orthodox church on Ponca Street were the only places she could go without a chaperone.

Leini was as frustrated in her idling as her guardians were happy to see her at leisure; a bookworm beauty tired of saving nickels for trips she would never be allowed to take; reading English as good or better than most anyone the Ralphs knew who was born here.

(Escape masquerading as leisure and the ability to read English better than anyone born along the Baltimore waterfront not quite the feat the Ralphs imagined.)

Leini's left hand bare on her seventeenth birthday, but just barely.

The wet hens harshly yoked—Greek maidens who'd arrived before Leini; the feather-plucking Esthers along Lombard Street as well as debutantes of the bluest Baltimore blood—all swore that affection simply grows and one day you no longer despise your husband's shaving mug, his elbows, or his spoon.

One day, they promised, you wake up and know love.

The cow bell on the front door of Ralph's clanged, bringing Leini back from Pamplona to the foot of Clinton Street.

A man about whom stories were told was coming her way.

Sometimes, Leini had heard, Orlo Pound wandered all the way down to the strawberry patches of Anne Arundel County.

Nibbling a bowl of pig's feet as she read, using her tongue to sort gristle from meat, Leini pushed a pebble of cartilage out of her mouth and wiped her fingers on a napkin.

Orlo took a seat cater-corner from her and took a good, long look—short hair, black as an olive, pale skin, and an innocent neck—before the teenager took a good look herself and went back to her book.

No one would ever see Greek in Orlo—it wasn't to be found in the great-great-grandson of Limey shipbuilders who'd settled on the Baltimore waterfront before the Revolution—but you couldn't help seeing the fun in him, the good.

"Hello Orlo," said Mrs. Ralph, setting down his beer, hand on her hip. "How is life in the world of junk?"

Leini moved closer for the answer and Orlo smiled at her through the frame made by the crook of Mrs. Ralph's arm.

"People still throwing away fortunes," he said. "This morning I found Mark Twain's typewriter."

"*Thisavros*," smiled Mrs. Ralph, who didn't know Mark Twain from Mark Trail. "What can I get for you, Mr. Lucky Man?"

Nodding toward Leini, he said: "The pig's feet look awfully good."

Leini blushed from her chest to her scalp.

Mark Twain's typewriter!

Hadn't she cut her hair in a bob without asking anyone's permission?

Taken to using "chap" and "rather" with her girlfriends?

Started scratching out a novel at the little saloon table next to her bed?

Leini jumped up.

"I'll get it," she said.

"Dig down good, Eleini," said Mrs. Ralph, walking behind the counter. "There's a little left on the bottom."

"That's the beauty part," said Orlo, watching Leini walk to the kitchen, black shoes and white socks below her apron strings; nudging Mr. Ralph out of the way to ladle out the last of the day's special.

She came back with a bowl piled high and steaming, her pulse racing.

The Ralphs' pig's feet were the best on the waterfront, bar none the best; even the grave-diggers said so; fat trotters of gelatinous pork butchered fresh on Goose Hill, boiled tender, brushed with melted lard and rolled in bread crumbs and fennel before crackling in the broiler.

Today, Mr. Ralph had made them the way Leini liked best:

marinated in a caper vinaigrette and simmered in a thin broth of tomato and basil.

"Tell me," she said to the junk man as he ate, "about Mark Twain's typewriter."

(We can trust him, thought Mrs. Ralph—an old woman admiring a young woman's verve—Mr. Ralph at the stationary tubs in the back, elbow deep in the pot from which the last of the pig's feet had come.)

Orlo pointed to Leini's book with his fork.

"Good stuff," he said.

"You know it?" she asked.

What didn't Orlo know?

Basement cleaner, alley creeper, and attic sweeper with freedom so far beyond the common man as to be understood only by derelicts and carnival workers.

He wandered for miles in search of treasure in the rags he baled for the Schmata Kings of New York, treasure glittering in the debris of other people's lives.

(The beauty part.)

When he arrived late to estate sales, after the vultures who circled the obituaries had made off with jewelry and furniture, Orlo would bargain the doors off the hinges and the stained glass from the transoms.

"You don't have to leave home to find adventure," said Orlo, and before he could address the question of Twain's typewriter—before Leini could remind him that she'd left her home long ago—a kid named Girlie Schuefel sauntered in with a parrot on her shoulder to fetch her family's dinner.

"How 'bout some of them good feet, Miss R?"

"Sorry, Girlie," said Mrs. Ralph. "We just sold out."

In the weeks after he met Leini, Orlo could not shake the picture of her pulling the string that held the pig knuckles together through the space between her front teeth.

"Can you meet me?"

"Yes."

"Where?"

"I'll find you."

Inventing ways to share crocks of pig's feet cooked as no one had ever cooked them; insane love—celibate and clandestine—until the Ralphs got wise and married Leini off with as much care as you'd use to chop pickles for tuna salad.

Orlo watched the ceremony from the roof of the Salvage House; the same spot where he sat and watched the firemen hose down the rubble of Ralph's a week later.

Our lives made up of could have beens, not *should* have beens.

Their hearts crippled by the fire that destroyed their livelihood, Mr. and Mrs. Ralph were soon buried, leaving Leini alone with a husband she despised and a lover she only saw in secret.

Who said they had pig's feet every time?

Sometimes they sat at the end of Orlo's pier and split an orange as the sun set over the harbor, the junkman holding the fruit against the sky before Leini peeled it with her thumb.

Or walked together without speaking.

More than once they ate hamburgers and pretended they were like everyone else.

Up on Eastern Avenue, the Great Bolewicki Depression Clock chimed: "It's not too late...it's only the Last Supper of Orlo and Leini."

Leini got off the bus at the corner of Clinton and Boston for the long walk down to the water and the sagging shipyard mansion with a single word white-washed across the side: SALVAGE.

By late 1978, Orlo's ancestral home was the only building still standing on Goose Hill from the old days; for years its doors had not opened on the bazaar that had brought generations of Baltimoreans—from the flappers to the freaks—down to the end of Clinton Street.

Even the Goose Hill branch of the Pratt Library was a memory, its patrons gone to television and the suburbs.

It had been much easier for Orlo and Leini to keep their secret in the past decade, from the day Leini's husband fired a gun into his mouth and society began caring less and less about who came and went from where.

Now they could walk the streets holding hands if they wanted; two old people too old for anyone to notice or care.

Easier, but not half the fun.

Aside from the spinsters who fed wild cats, most of the people who came to the crumbling seawall were lost in their own affairs, and the others—ship spotters and kite fliers—took Orlo and Leini for siblings.

Leini walked without a cane, turning her back to the street when trucks rumbled by: loud, dirty monsters that in one lifetime had replaced ships and trains as the way to move cargo in the United States.

"There goes Old Lady Leini," said a teenager riding a skateboard, a girl alongside of him balancing on what was left of the curb. "My grandmother says she and the junkman have been doing it since Babe Ruth was in reform school."

"So?" said the girl, admiring Leini's shoes.

"So everybody knows. Her husband caught them together in the bathtub and blew his brains out. It's the oldest story on the Hill."

"So good for them," said the girl, running off into a sharp wind.

The cold cut through Leini's coat as she rapped on the door of the Salvage House. Orlo kissed her dry lips and hung her coat on the horns of a billy goat, another denizen of Clinton Street survived by Orlo's junk and little else.

Everything the junkman owned had belonged to someone else before it belonged to him: the chairs he sat in, the bed he slept in, the pots he cooked in.

Back when he kept fish, the bowl they swam in.

"Something smells good," said Leini. "Something I've tasted before?"

"How would you know?" he answered.

(We know by tiny receptors like the transistor radios on which Orlo made a fortune in the early '60s; you can still see mental patients walking down Pratt Street with them, box radios in jackets of perforated leather. Receptors deep in the nose bond to gas molecules to send signals to the olfactory bulb and the bulb's nerves trip circuits behind a screen in the brain where precise firing patterns {meatloaf in the shape of a rectangle and pig's feet a spinning top}—reveal what smells so good.

Or not so.

Smell is keenest in childhood, followed by a long leveling that lasts through late middle age before dropping so sharply that an eighty-one-year-old man has only half the power of a girl drinking in the bouquet of adventure for the first time.)

"Little Leini wants to help you straighten this place up," said Leini, stepping through the junk on her way to the kitchen. "She thinks you'd be a rich man if you knew what you've got."

"You see what I got," said Orlo.

Leini stopped at a vanity, one thin drawer on each side of the small table and curved wings of leaded milk glass attached to an oval mirror.

Its finish, once blond, was black now from a sticky lacquer that had settled over the house in Orlo's refusal to cover his frying pan when he cooked.

On the vanity lay a piece Leini had never seen, a wooden box with an old map of the Holy Land carved in the lid—coordinates that once stretched to the four corners reduced to a thin blue band around the harbor rim, boundaries that shrank with every rape and murder and drug addict telling her three-year-old to shut the fuck up.

Leini lifted the lid and pan-pipes began to play, her mind giving words to the melody.

The Ballad of Orlo and Leini.

"Let's eat," she said, closing the lid.

Orlo set a stew pot on the table alongside a wheel of bread, and with a ladle he'd recovered from the rubble of Ralph's—cleaning it up and forging a new handle—he scooped out a pair of fatty knuckles dripping a thin red sauce of tomato and basil; serving Leini and then himself.

"To you," he said, raising a glass of water. "Who makes me new every week."

Years of such weeks, coming together on playgrounds, beaches, and rooftops, by the side of the road and in open fields; blankets doubling as tablecloth and bed sheet.

They'd made fires where none had burned since the meteor showers to cook in combinations no one had ever tried: sweet digits of swine melting in the blood of ducks, hiding under black pools of squid ink, bobbing through tureens of clear consommé.

In a corner of the Salvage House basement, where he once canned peaches and steamed bushels of crabs, Orlo kept a bank of oak filing cabinets that City Hall had unloaded after World War II.

The cabinets were fat with envelopes, old bags and scraps of paper covered in the scrawl of five languages, two of them dead; handwriting that explained how to make sauces to seduce the long-seduced; recipes from newspapers and housewives and the memories of itinerant cooks all jumbled together with experiments from the tip of Orlo's tongue.

On top of the first cabinet sat a dirt-choked typewriter that Twain had never seen, the machine on which Leini had pecked three half-baked and unfinished novels before telling Orlo to get rid of it.

Shelves lined a wall across from the cabinets and on them Orlo would let fruit age until the moment before ripe turned to rot—red and black currants, pears for cooking with honey, and rows of melons; shelves littered now with dried seed.

On a third wall: round, sandstone jars for salt pork from which, early this morning, Orlo removed a half-dozen pig's feet, soaked them all day and rubbed them with crushed bay leaf.

Leini pulled the string that held those knuckles together and slid it across her tongue.

"Something new?"

Leini could turn two eggs and a piece of cheese into a meal; a lifetime of singing the "Come In My Kitchen Blues" teaching her to make do, not with anything, but nothing: peeling fresh walnuts from Druid Hill Park until her fingers turned yellow, meals that cost no more than the effort it took to bend down and pick up.

"Something old," said Orlo.

"I know this sauce."

"It's Ralph's," said Orlo. "I made him recite it to me after the fire. I make it for myself when I can't see you."

Leini's own kitchen on Ponca Street was efficiently American and nothing more, for on the calendar of illicit feast days, there is no such thing as a moderate oven.

"But I'm here," said Leini, tearing off a piece of bread for a man who would be dead of bad valves and pig fat before the night was out. "I'm right here."

Leini had never been chased by the bulls of Pamplona, attended a ballgame much less a ball, or returned to Greece for the funerals of her parents.

The excitement of finding treasure that others could not see was as close as she'd gotten to the stories she loved, and it was not lost on her that the author who had beguiled her youth—a tough guy who presumed to know how every story turned out—had blown his head off while Helen Keller died like an angel in her sleep.

With Orlo's mourners behind her, Leini bit deep into her orange and let the juice run down her chin, wondering how much time would pass before she joined her lover.

As she stared across the channel, a red tug with a white dot on its stack pulled near and she saw Ace Gentile at the wheel of the *Resolute*.

The Ace had treated the junkman and his lover to long and aimless rides around the harbor on many an afternoon.

Like so many of Orlo and Leini's protectors, the tug captain did so not just because he was fond of Orlo, but because he got something he needed by being close to his friend's story.

Remember that time?

Who could forget?

We talk about it to this day.

Leini waved as the *Resolute* blew Orlo a long and shrill farewell, a black wreath on her bow, an empty barge in tow.

Our lady of opportunity with a stucco cone of light . . .

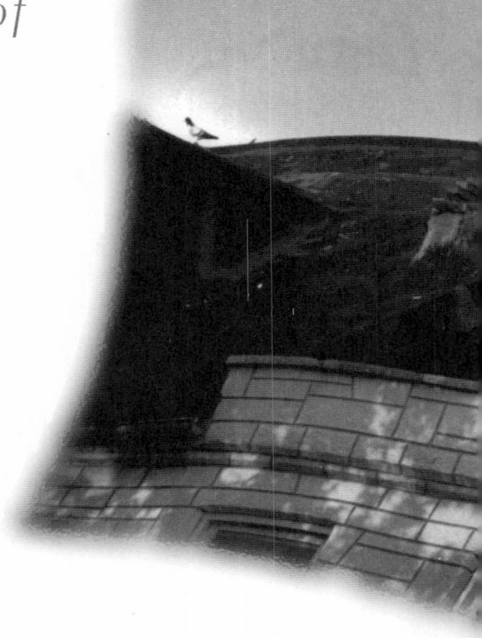

Orlo's Velvet Room

Leini stepped off the streetcar as late September broke over the Holy Land, a rope and canvas shopping bag in one hand, a book under her arm with an address penciled inside the cover.

Below a black house dress, she wore white socks and old shoes; at the bottom of the sack that smelled of onions lay an evening dress with evening a dozen hours away.

Passing Prevas Brothers' lunch counter, Leini gave the diner stools a turn; one after the other, six stools revolving behind her as she swept into the Broadway Market, swinging her satchel like a school kid.

Striding past the butcher, Leini made her way to the flower stall for carnations, red and white like the flag above the Polish Home dance hall, a fun house of beer and clarinets to which Leini had never been; not because she wasn't Polish (in 1929 it only seemed like everyone along the Baltimore waterfront had been born in Krakow, the same way the radio made folks believe everyone but them was rich); but because in her twenty years—long enough to be married and miserable and a mother—Leini had never been to any event that wasn't sponsored by the Greek Orthodox Church and chaperoned by a thousand sets of eyes.

Before today, she'd never ventured beyond her own neighborhood with money and a purpose all her own.

Leini bowed to her bouquet as she left the market and an Old Country shrew—dressed exactly like Leini but four times older—stopped hosing down the sidewalk to let her pass.

Finnish sailors stood in boarding house doorways sipping coffee, divining Leini's form beneath her costume, savoring it. Ducks and hens squawked from coops. The birds would be killed today and eaten tomorrow. It was Friday.

Lakeins had wedding rings on special but it was too beautiful a morning for a married girl pretending to be a widow to stop and admire them.

Turning at Eastern Avenue toward downtown, Leini followed her instructions to a narrow alley of crackerbox rowhouses and was just about to duck down the lane when she noticed a man leaving morning Mass approach a rummy rooting through a trash barrel.

Reaching into his pocket, the do-gooder jumped back when the derelict raised a broken bottle.

"Come on St. Francis. Try and give me a dollar. I'll knock your teeth out. How about your roadster and your Victrola and your gin? Just try it."

Gripping her flowers, Leini raced down an alley just wide enough for a horse and wagon to rattle by; down to a house whose number she'd committed to heart.

Only two of her neighbors on Ponca Street had Victrolas, roadsters were pictures in magazines, and—with or without Prohibition—she would not have known gin from ginger ale.

All Leini knew were Greeks willing to work themselves to death to afford things they had no intention of buying.

"Only one reality," raged the rag picker. "Shit and Spirit...fish and swine under the same God..."

Deep in the alley, Leini calmed herself and remembered to take a tunnel that divided 408 Cabbage Alley from 410.

Trembling as she ducked into the arched passageway, Leini was struck dumb by the drunkard's prophecy of false prosperity and a shower of Fatima sunshine at the end of the tunnel.

Forcing herself to slow down, she considered what had delivered her to this hour and realized for the first time that it was not love. Her life could not have been what her *mitera* and *patera* wanted when they shipped the smartest girl their village had ever known to live with trusted friends in America.

Leini had wanted to be a scholar.

A teacher.

A librarian at least.

Fear led me here, she decided, scooting down a tunnel so narrow that her elbows scraped the walls.

Other people's fear.

Her guardians had forced her into marriage with a man she did not know because they saw the way her tongue filled the gap between her teeth when the junkman came around.

They were terrified that she would find a penis before she found the altar.

"Life is not what you find in your storybooks," preached the woman who'd raised her.

"Then where do stories come from?"

"Oh, my ripe little fig," the woman laughed, squeezing Leini's shoulders as they scrubbed pots. "They make them up."

Leini stepped out of the tunnel and into a garden made of two yards cobbled together, a small, lush park with rosebushes and canopies of fruit trees growing from whiskey barrels sawed in half.

A massive Star of David loomed from a brick wall at the back of the yard, ivy reaching up for it from a cast-iron bathtub filled with dirt.

Moving toward the Star, Leini saw it was made from broken diner china, a mosaic of shattered cups and saucers rimmed with thin bands of green.

Climbing onto the lip of the tub, feeling it wobble beneath her, Leini touched the shards with her palm—smooth here and jagged there—and it reminded her of the wolf in the book she'd brought.

"A flat-nosed Jew with two fine growths of hair luxuriating in each nostril...his cufflinks made of human molars."

Hopping down, she looked around at the high brick walls ringing the garden and felt safe.

No one, she thought, knows that I'm here.

Turning the knob on a door left open for her, Leini entered a large kitchen made from two smaller ones, the fire wall between 408 and 410 removed, the space filled with the warmth of an absent family and their recent breakfast.

A soiled bib hung over the back of a highchair, dirty dishes were stacked in a sink beneath a window looking out on the garden; spice grew on the sill.

"If there is a royalty among herbs, Eleini reigns sovereign...no other is so revered for its indelible beauty and stubborn fragrance..."

Leini picked a baby's bowl from the sink, ran a finger around its rim and licked cold farina from her pinky. Turning to a pinched set of wooden steps behind the coal stove—every angle at ninety, tighter than the tunnel—Leini began to climb, her bag squashed against cracked and curving plaster as she rose beyond the second floor to a splintered, scarlet door at the top.

A pair of work boots stood outside the door, wool socks stuffed inside cracked leather. Leini knelt to undo her shoes, left them and her socks alongside the other pair and stood.

Stretching her toes, she closed her eyes, exhaled, opened her eyes, knocked, and waited.

"You made it," said Orlo, pulling Leini in, his lover moving barefoot across yards of new velvet the hue of a koala's coat; fingers reaching for walls draped with velvet the tint of the quiver between her legs; deep maroon pleated like the flesh below the eyes of women from lands that demanded such lights be veiled.

Velvet beyond Leini's reach as Orlo brought her to the bed; spinning in the long, narrow room, arms slipping from her coat, flowers falling to the floor.

"Orlo," she said. "My God, Orlo, give me a minute to look."

Eyehooks snagged, buttons popped, and Leini's head hung over the side of the bed for an up-ended view of the marvelous secret.

At the far end of the room—near windows that had looked out onto Cabbage Alley before Orlo bricked them up and hung Kelly velvet where the frames used to be—the morning sun warmed a skylight paned with green and purple glass.

Tumbling from the bed to move her arms against the carpet, Leini asked: "Where are we?"

"Alone," said Orlo, falling on top of her.

All alone inside a bruised membrane of sweet and sorrowful velvet, purple streaked with gray and gold in the upper room of a crooked alley house a century old: twelve feet wide and twenty-seven feet long from front to back.

Orlo kissed Leini's collarbone, ran his thumbs along her ribs and dipped his chin between them, measuring the length of each curved bone with the tip of his nose as she stared up at beams lacquered like tree bark, her skirt in a corner.

Two floors below, a door opened and Leini felt the creak of its hinges along her spine as Orlo set his mouth on hers.

Sunshine poured down from the skylight. Leini flipped onto her stomach and crawled toward it.

Buckets of color, she thought, velvet smooth against her stomach; gallons of color drenching my body if I made it happen down there.

Reaching after her, Orlo saw money pinned to the inside of Leini's black slip as she wriggled free of it, a pair of twenties and a clutch of fives and tens fastened with a diaper pin; money skimmed from her milk and butter purse over long weeks of perfect waiting.

Purple on my neck, she thought, inching toward the light in her bra and panties; Orlo reaching for her calves.

Green on my feet.

Orlo balled up the slip and tossed it aside.

Gold stenciled on my nipples like grape leaves.

Sliding out of his pants, Orlo laughed as he caught Leini under the light; pulling himself onto his lover's back like a sea turtle; her skin smoother than the carpet.

Orlo rested against Leini until she turned to face him, color speckling the dark crescents below her eyes.

Purple and green floating in the space between her front teeth; pink tongue filling the gap.

"It's beautiful," she said, spilling tears a bookworm cries out of a loneliness that books cannot relieve; the tears of an innocent who's been yoked and bridled and slaughtered upon an altar of pride.

A good mother ashamed of resenting motherhood.

An angry wife fucked for two-and-a-half years, about to make love for the first time.

"I'll do it," Leini whispered, pastel sunshine blinding eyes that could at last bear to open during sex. "I will leave tonight."

Orlo could not hear her for the sound of the blood pumping through thighs warm and close against the sides of his head, his teeth in purple so dark it edged on brown.

Turning her head from side to side in rhythm with the junkman's tongue, Leini spied her black widow's disguise in a heap across the room and tried to hide her tears.

Until her seventeenth summer, when the junkman found her ladling out bowls of pig's feet down at the end of Clinton Street, Leini's guardians believed her only fault was reading too many books.

And then they caught her holding Orlo's hand as they cruised the alleys for junk and declared that it was time; arrangements for the preservation of her honor—canned preserves on a pantry shelf—made with less care than it took to chop pickles for tuna salad.

Come, pleaded Orlo the night before her wedding.

Come, go with me.

"Come here," said Leini, wiping her eyes and pulling Orlo up, ashamed of boo-hooing in the midst of such pleasure.

Just run, she thought as Orlo moved inside of her by degrees so small they could only be measured by touch.

And when the perforations in the film joined the teeth of the sprocket, Leini saw a strobe flicker inside the skylight and glimpsed a raisin lost in white sheets.

She saw Mrs. Ralph on her death bed.

Holding onto the girl's arm with a promise to save her a spot in the world to come, the woman who'd guided Leini from schoolgirl to housewife sent her sweet fig away with pursed lips and regrets; Mrs. Ralph's last moments vexed by Leini's fate like no other indiscretion from her long life; the obsession to control another's fate the only sin that would not yield to the oil of the priest who'd come by with the magic words.

Leini left the dying woman's side to sit on the stairs above the bed, laying her head against the banister as Mrs. Ralph used the last of her strength to summon her husband.

Not for a sip of water or another pillow.

To demand: "How long did you look?"

"Easy," said Mr. Ralph. "Go easy."

But she would go in anger; no longer sorry that God had never given them a child of their own.

"How many coffee shops before you found that Satan George?"

Mr. Ralph remembered the urgency of the summer when every alarm in the house went off; he knew that his wife had been every bit as upset as he and pushed him hard to do something until George appeared in the smoke made when fear and pride are rubbed together.

With her last breath, she said: "Help Leini get away."

Leini's sobs filled the stairway with tears more hot and full than the ones absorbed by velvet now that she was finally joined to the man she loved.

"Orlo," she moaned. "Or...lo."

Less than a month after his wife passed, Mr. Ralph would be dead too.

Orlo pulled on his underpants and opened the spigots on the tub as Leini waited for her bath; tub and bed so close that a man stretched out in one could kiss a woman sprawled across the other without straining his neck.

While Orlo fiddled with the faucets—not knowing how hot Leini liked her bath, whether she washed with a cloth or a sponge, or, until today, that her breasts disappeared when she lay on her back—Leini ran her hands along the walls for her first good look around the room.

One long, narrow room from the front of the house to the back: a skylight, a small bed, a tub, and a pair of French doors opening onto a balcony above the garden.

Velvet walls, velvet bed, and velvet floor; velvet stained beneath the skylight.

The whole of this fantastic, clandestine cell; a svelte room could have been sparer still, just space enough for Orlo to arch the soles of his feet while Leini touched her palms to the floor.

Circling the room until she came upon the tub—jet black hull above crimson feet—Leini saw the pressure drop in the spigot and knew someone was downstairs.

"Who lives here?"

"People who save coal in the summer by putting their bath water out in the yard to warm in the sun," said Orlo.

"Besides them."

"Whores, hillbillies, and *mavri*," said Orlo. "Packing house ladies and oyster shuckers."

"Who lives in this house?"

"The Pinchereles. Paul and Teddy."

"Artists?"

"Heroes."

"Both of them?"

"Hardheads," said Orlo, shaking powdered soap beneath the spigot. "Teddy cores pineapples down Lord Mott's. The knives cut her hands and the acid seeps in. She has to wear white gloves because they're always infected."

"Him?"

"Harbor rat. Obsessed with living as they please."

Bubbles rose in the tub and Leini laughed beyond her age, leaning on Orlo's shoulder as she stepped into the tub.

"No one lives as they please."

"Teddy works at the packing house only when she has to," said Orlo. "Paul crabs in the summer and sails cook when a tug heads down to Norfolk. Sometimes he takes women out to ships on anchor. Dreamed of working the river back home, he was going to be the Jewish Mark Twain, but they don't let Yids pilot the Mississippi."

"The Star," said Leini, sliding down, water and foam spilling over the sides as her body filled the tub. "What's his wife?"

"Agnes Theodora Zaminski."

"Polack?"

"No, Len, she's Greek," laughed Orlo, lathering soap into her hair. "She's got some kind of nerve for a kid from Binney Street. The Warsaw monsters from St. Casimir's tie their ornery kids to railings with wet clothesline and leave 'em screaming as the rope dries. You think her family wasn't good and pissed off when she married a dago-Jew from New Orleans dark enough to pass for colored?"

Dark enough.

Light enough.

Good enough.

Bad enough.

"Mad as hell," said Orlo. "And you know what? *Her* family got over it."

And they're not Greek, thought Leini, slipping below the water.

Leini had not heard her parents' voices for more than eleven years, yet succumbed—out of fear that they would never speak to her again—to the mores of an extended family that reached anywhere in the world where some stubble-chinned Nick flipped eggs on a grill.

Orlo dumped a handful of cold water on Leini's head.

"Jesus Christ," said Leini.

"Paul and Teddy are exiles," said Orlo. "They pay the price."

"More than us?"

"They're together. Paul's prudent—when he wants to know what time it is he asks somebody—and Teddy would bite a quarter before she'd squander it."

"I saw a bum this morning," said Leini, rinsing her hair beneath the spigot. "Someone tried to give him some money and he went crazy."

"See 'em every day," said Orlo. "Him and the other smokehounds hang around the car shop waiting for the boy to crack the denatured alcohol. They come with their cups and their pennies. For a nickel they could have a glass of beer, but they want poison on the barrel. Pissing their pants and going blind."

"But he wouldn't take a dollar bill."

"Some people you can't help," said Orlo, wringing the wash cloth. "Did you see the pig?"

"Don't start."

"On the side of the slaughterhouse across the street. I'm sure it watched you come down the alley."

"Who watched me?"

"A concrete pig, Len. Teddy sculpted it in exchange for a lifetime of scraps," said Orlo, lusting for the delicacy they'd shared so long in celibacy. "Feet, tails, ears. Ever eat a sow's ear? You suck the meat from the husks like an artichoke heart."

Orlo took Leini's head and in his hands and held it absolutely still.

"Listen," he said. "They're running a herd through the alley. Don't get no fresher than meat on the hoof."

"Poison on the barrel," said Leini.

"I made our meal for Paul and Teddy once."

Our ball, thought Leini.

Our chain.

"Like it ain't never been made before," said Orlo. "Pig's feet and black linguini."

"Not today," said Leini. "Today we're going to eat like normal people."

"You use squid ink to dye the pasta. I simmered the trotters with tripe and celery, spent an hour skimming off the fat while the knuckles dissolved."

"Why are you telling me this?"

"Because it made me feel better on a bad day."

"This is a good day."

"It was sundown on a Friday, Paul and Teddy were fixing their Sabbath meal and I was headed for another weekend alone. I'd spent all day hauling these tubs from uptown, squeezing them in here without destroying them."

Leini pictured the tub in the backyard—the one turned into a flower pot—and wondered how much dirt it would take to bury her in it.

"I wasn't going to mope through your alley again on the chance I might see you doing dishes at the sink."

Orlo felt Leini's muscles tighten beneath the washcloth as he scrubbed between the wings of her shoulders.

And you don't know, she thought, how many clean dishes I stood there washing.

"Teddy was playing with cement in the garden, watching me," said Orlo. "She said I was walking sad and invited me to stay for dinner. I hated them feeling sorry for me and offered to cook. We talked as I made the meal and I told her everything but your name."

Black linguini.

And pig's feet simmered down with tripe and lemon.

Cartilage on top of spaghetti.

All covered with cheese.

Love.

"Paul brought me up here after dinner," said Orlo, standing to get a towel. "They'd just bought the building and it wasn't nothing but crumbling plaster and cobwebs. You couldn't walk across the floor."

Leini looked at the skylight and thought of leaping through it; that maybe she could rise up on her will, break the glass with her head, and shake the shards from her ankles as she flew away.

Leini yanked the plug and the drain gulped bath water as she searched for the opening in Orlo's shorts, savoring one of the delicacies she refused her husband.

Clearing her throat, she asked: "The Jew ate pig's feet?"

"When his plate was clean," said Orlo. "He leaned across the table and licked the fat from his wife's fingers."

Two houses and itching for a third.

Eight short weeks after Orlo and Leini made love for the first time in a room swathed in velvet, Paul Pincherele would write his kin to see if there was work down South and room for three.

Soon he'd be grateful for shelter.

And by the time auctioneers were barking numbers outside of a secret jewel along an obscure alley on the Baltimore waterfront, more than thirteen million Americans would be dying for work.

They had done as they pleased.

They were living pretty good in this country.

Orlo's semen swirled down the drain with Leini's saliva and the junkman soaped a cloth to wipe the silver lining it left behind.

Kneeling, Orlo turned the spigot on full and warm and put his head beneath it, his words bouncing off the porcelain and ringing in his ears; light from the afternoon sun pouring in from the balcony, sparkling through the water streaming down his back.

"When I was little, in the summertime," he said, "my mother would punch holes in the bottom of a coffee can, hang it from a nail on the back of our house and run a hose through it for a sprinkler. That's how we had our fun."

Stretched out on the bed—spread like a kid pretending to be a starfish—Leini remembered the Mediterranean of her backyard and octopus boiled in kettles on the beach, no one but little Greeks for friends.

She pulled down the velvet bedspread and slipped beneath the sheets with Orlo's voice in her ears: how he was descended from the original shipbuilders of Baltimore; how the idea to trade in junk came to him in a doughboy trench he'd shared with a tough nut named Abe Sherman, knowing he could sell long-coats and motorcycle guts after the Armistice the way Sherman hawked newspapers at the foot of the Battle Monument.

"Abe's good to me," said Orlo. "Got me a deal on all of this velvet from a dressmaker on Paca Street."

Scoop up the baby and go, thought Leini, humming herself to sleep below the murmur of her lover's memories.

"I can see the Statue of Liberty atop the roof of the ice cream factory, but I cannot see the world inside this velvet cell..."

Leini woke before Orlo and slipped from his arm.

She moved quietly around the darkening room, picking up her clothes and gathering wilted carnations. Taking fresh clothes from her sack, she dressed without a mirror, brushed her teeth in the tub, and walked barefoot onto the balcony, black hair still damp from the bath.

Moving from warm velvet to cold tile, Leini thought of all the nickels she'd saved for a day she never thought would come; pleased with the conversion of sacrifice and coins from her husband's drinking pants—any pants on any day—into the ways and means for a day to remember.

"Just like the artists," she thought, leaning with pleasure on a railing cast in grapevines, face open to the setting sun.

(Paul Pincherele pleased himself believing that the wrought iron trellised across his beloved New Orleans had sprouted like native fauna and Orlo had put up a Bourbon Street railing on the Velvet Room balcony to make the expatriate feel better about the choices he'd made. But nearly all of the Crescent City's gingerbread had been cast in Baltimore and the junkman never let Pincherele forget it.)

Down in the garden, the woman for whom Paul had forsaken his hometown sat in the garden with a book, nude, Leini noticed, from the waist up; a pineapple slicing sculptor confident enough to expose her nipples to the daylight, turning the pages with fingers scarred from coring knives.

"That could be me," thought Leini, reaching inside her gown to touch breasts no different—except for fresh teeth marks—than when she was fourteen; no match for the heavy, pale globes of the Pole reading below shimmering triangles of David made from shattered china and splintered wishbones.

Teddy caressed her nipples with each turned page and Leini imitated her with fingertips still puckered from the bath.

Teddy was plain and Leini was beautiful.

Teddy made art out of nothing while Leini read the same books over and over for the parts she missed.

Teddy content as the dying sun made the Star rotate on the wall above her.

Leini anxious—"What does she know that I don't?"—with the knowledge that stories fail because they leave so much out.

In the time it would take for her to pull on stockings and buckle her shoes, she and Orlo could be in a taxi headed uptown before the orchestras began to play.

The doors behind Leini opened and Orlo joined her on the balcony, bare-chested and barefoot, rope holding up a pair of clean work pants; his hair wet like hers and combed back like hers, just like hers except for blond curls springing free at the sides of his head.

Holding the hem of Leini's dress, pinching it like worry beads, Orlo tried to shake the nightmare that had woken him.

"Is that her?" asked Leini.

"Yes."

Leaning back against Orlo, she said: "Look how she sits."

"Like what?"

"Out in the open like that. Naked," she said, moving Orlo's hand inside the front of her dress.

"Are you insane?" said Orlo, pulling his hand away. "Look again."

Paul walked out of the house with the baby in his arms and Teddy closed her book. Sitting the boy on a straight-backed wooden chair in the middle of the garden, Paul took scissors and a comb from his pocket and Teddy knelt next to the child to keep him still.

Paul combed the kid's hair down to the tip of his nose, snipping swiftly as Teddy steadied the boy with whispers.

"First haircut," said Orlo and Leini pictured one just like it except that the parent doing the cutting and the one doing the soothing were the same person.

(Because her own life seemed so hard, Leini assumed it was easier for other people. But this, she thought, watching the Pinchereles, is a couple we can be ourselves with.)

Slipping the shears in his pocket, Paul brushed away the trimmings and Teddy pressed a curled lock between the pages of her book.

Teddy spread a white cloth over a table near the fountain—water bubbling from the brush of a young artist cast in concrete before an easel—and set the table. Paul picked the last tomatoes of summer and green peppers turning red.

"When they bought this place," said Orlo, "that yard was nothing but dog shit and cement."

"You told me."

Factory whistles cut across the rooftops and Leini felt the city come alive for the second time that day.

"Let's go dancing."

"In a horse and wagon?"

"A Yellow cab."

"Where?"

"Johnson's Mecca," said Leini, running down speakeasies she'd heard salesmen talk about at the diner. "Sis's Hole. The Eagle in Bolton Hill."

"You know these places?"

"Drinks on the roof of the Southern Hotel," she grinned. "My treat."

A block away on Caroline Street, light glowed from a Statue of Liberty atop the Tutti Frutti Ice Cream Company; Our Lady of Opportunity raising a scoop of electric light in a stucco cone.

Orlo took a peach and a penknife from his pocket, cut a slice and slipped it into his mouth, talking with food in his mouth.

"Hold on to your money."

Leini tried to speak again and Orlo filled her mouth with peach. She chewed, swallowed, and started over.

"Let's celebrate."

Orlo plucked the pit free with the tip of his knife and sucked it clean.

"Celebrate what?" he asked, spitting the pit over the side of the balcony.

Until Orlo fell through the gap in Leini's teeth, Mr. Ralph and his wife had loved their junk-collecting neighbor like a son.

Could they not have waited to see how it would turn out before hating him as one?

Looking up, the junkman peered over the garden wall to see Nilo the Knife Man pushing his grinding stone back to the sheds of Monkey Row. Over the long, brutal years ahead, Nilo would build a clock above a Highlandtown appliance store that would exhort a generation to hope.

"It's not too late..."

But today the Great Depression was just a bank of dark clouds sailing toward an ice cream cone's neon glow.

"The first king of Mardi Gras was a Jew, Len," said Orlo as Paul built a fire in a shallow pit bordered by flat rocks; Teddy walking out of the house with a rockfish on a tray, the baby toddling behind with napkins. "Paul's an apostate."

"How so?"

"He stood in front of a crucifix, said 'I do,' and promised to raise his children Catholic."

"And?"

"And I'm not leaving Baltimore."

Leini turned to look at the man who'd spent a thousand hours carting the Jazz Age to Cabbage Alley for her; searching unpaved roads to rescue a diaspora of junk a contented soul would have no reason to seek; miles of velvet equal to one long day of sex and cowardice.

Folks who soon would not have a pot to piss in were tossing away fortunes.

The five-sided skylight came from the back of a Lithuanian pool hall near Mencken's house; the French doors Orlo discovered face down under a pile of cardboard on Eutaw Street and the stained-glass transom that now shimmered above them was snatched from the house of a red-headed trouble-maker on Dillon Street who traded it for a case of beer.

Orlo replaced the house number—2729—with letters spelling his lover's name.

"I only asked to go dancing," said Leini.

In the garden, Paul rubbed the fish with olive oil and rosemary and slipped it on the searing grate; fire crackling and the scent of silver skin crisping to black wafting up to the balcony.

"Then let's go down and join them."

"We haven't been invited."

"What if we'd had ka-ka and onions the first day we met?" said Leini, a ballroom of jazz in her head shrinking to a closet of blues. "Would we be eating that for the rest of our lives?"

"Come on Len," said Orlo. "You can buy a month of groceries with the money you brought."

"Yeah," said Leini. "I could."

Paul brought the fish to the table, a spatula under the head, the tail pinched between his fingers. Teddy made the sign of the cross and Paul covered his eyes in silent prayer until she was done, knowing just how long it took her to bless the meal.

"I thought you said they did as they pleased," Leini snapped.

Teddy trickled olive oil over a bowl of boiled potatoes and Paul took the spatula to the fish like a knife, cutting off the head and setting it on the side for himself.

"This is our Paris," said Orlo, suddenly contrite, kissing Leini's neck. "Our New York. Our Jerusalem. That famous painting downtown? It's not called 'The Fountain of Constantinople.'"

Teddy worked through the fish with the tips of her fingers, picking out the bones before bringing it to her baby's mouth. The kid spit the fish out, grabbed a handful of potatoes from his mother's plate, and threw it in the air.

Paul grabbed the boy's wrist and the child squirmed free, pointing at Orlo and Leini on the balcony.

"Leini...," Orlo implored.

"Don't talk."

A vague harbor breeze started in a corner of the yard where two walls met; dry bones flaking on the Star as seagulls gobbled wet bread in the gutter where Eastern Avenue spills into Cabbage Alley like scrub water.

A sullen mistress, Leini?

A librarian at the least.

"Your Baltimore is a nice secret," she said, brushing past Orlo to find her shoes, Mecca in her sights. "But I'm going back to Greece."

I want to be an American . . .

People Love Lies

"If it ain't decent and it ain't right,
stay the hell away from it..."
Virginia S. Baker, prophet

This is George's story and he would take it back if he could. On the Fourth of July in 1948—across a long weekend when Orlo and Leini ran off again to make love and eat pig's feet cooked as no one had made them before and the great Muddy Waters traveled to Baltimore to sing the blues in the basement of a Chinese laundry on Eastern Avenue—George Papageorgiou was losing the last part of his mind that worked.

The Fourth fell on a Sunday, the night Muddy and his band were booked into Spiro's Downbeat, a fat blue thumb throbbing amidst fish stalls, bakeries, tubs of olives and tanks of squid in a neighborhood where people raised their children not to act like Americans.

Two days before, Leini told George another dirty lie. Orlo hired a boy to look after the horse that pulled his wagon, and the lovers drifted down the Chesapeake with a weekend's change of clothes, a bag of lemons, and two dozen salted trotters.

Leaving George alone to hire half-a-dozen busted onions to spin the shimmy-shimmy-koko-bop in the middle of the night as he drank alone and played with himself in the Downbeat, trying not to think.

Now George was many things—itinerant seamen, petty thief, hopeless drunk and whore monger—but he wasn't important enough to be responsible for his wife's betrayals.

His shortcomings made it easy for Leini to sneak away, but he could never get drunk enough to ignore what he could not prove. And he was too ignorant to know that his demons would sprout like the dandelions Orlo and Leini picked for garnish if he buried a knife in the junkman's neck or emptied a pistol into his bride's drawers the way he'd wanted to for so long.

Just back-handing her wasn't doing it anymore.

About dawn, George slipped each of the dancers a bottle of booze, paid them out of petty cash Spiro used to fence stolen instruments, and shepherded his chorus line into cabs before passing out, naked except for white socks and brown shoes, cursing through spittle when the boss found him later in the morning.

Spiro held George's trousers in front of his right-hand-man's bloated face, an empty wallet dragging the pants down in the back.

"I know it," gurgled George in his stupor. "Like it crawled up my ass and died."

Spiro draped George's pants over his back and fetched him a glass of water, biting his tongue as he looked around at the mess, wondering what had been stolen and wishing the parade that had trooped through had taken their marshal with them.

Still, he was grateful for the chance to forgive his old friend such nights, more and more of these nights it seemed; glad for another opportunity to absolve himself of the alibis he afforded George's wife and her beloved junkman.

Spiro bore Orlo no ill, this American with the gift for finding treasure in debris. The junkman brought Spiro records most people didn't know existed, outfitting the Downbeat with the best colored jukebox between Richmond and Harlem.

No one in Baltimore had a copy of Muddy's "I Can't Be Satisfied."

The day it was released in Chicago a few months back it sold out before the sun went down. Yet Spiro had two: one for the box and one for his private collection.

For this and other favors the nightclub owner paid Orlo well.

"I see nothing," he told the junkman.

He told George the same thing.

Spiro put a glass of fizzing Bromo Seltzer under George's nose and kneaded his pale shoulders as morning light fell like a net across the black and white tiles on the dance floor.

"Easy, my friend," he whispered. "This is a big night for us. Who knows how big? The great Muddy Waters is coming here, right here George, to our club. Let me tell you about this black Hercules..."

Not again, thought George, unable to remember the face of a single woman from the night before; Leini's lies too good for him, lies mixed-up with too much truth; his hangover urging him to kill them both.

George missed his wife and had to shit so bad he feared messing himself.

"During the war, Alan Lomax decides he will be the one to find Robert Johnson," said Spiro, pulling a chair close. "But Robert is already gone, killed dead Georgie—poisoned by a jealous husband..."

"Please!" cried George.

"But Lomax didn't know. He went down to Mississippi with a record machine to search for a dead man. You should visit Mississippi George—out in the fields it is almost as beautiful as Greece except the sea is bright green. You'd be surprised how many Greeks have restaurants there. Robert Johnson cannot be found above the ground, but Lomax does not give up and people tell him: 'Bob's gone, but there's someone else...'"

Spiro brought his face close to George and purred: "He finds the great Muddy Waters riding on a tractor!"

"Please," begged George, pulling at the dark flesh under his eyes.

Spiro stood and spread his arms toward the stage where just a few hours ago a half-dozen naked women had taken turns sticking their tongues down each other's throats.

"Tonight...," he declared. "Muddy Waters will sing the blues here on Eastern Avenue and people will come from all over because Spiro Alatzas has told them it is a thing not to be missed."

Holy Mother of God, moaned George.

"The boys from the papers will be here, radio too. The word has gone out. Lee Halfpenny is bringing his best fighters and even Billie has called in to put her name on the list. Yes! Miss Holiday herself, and I need you, George, tonight of all nights, to clean up and pull yourself together."

George lifted his head and stared sideways.

"And every one-armed, wall-eyed, *skilo-mavros* loving freak in Baltimore."

Jumping up, he ran naked to stationary tubs at the back of the club and vomited, his bowels exploding with liquor and grease.

"Who gives a fuck?" he raged, the words bouncing between the smooth concrete walls of the tub and his ringing ears, his body smeared with filth and not enough orifices on his person for everything that wanted out. "For what? To hear a bunch of niggers sing with marbles in their mouths? Everybody makes their own trouble."

George heaved again and wiped his lips with the back of his hand.

"The fucking blues," he panted. "You're the only one who cares about that noise. Everybody on the block hates us for bringing coloreds up here and half the customers show up just to see if somebody's going to get stabbed."

George turned the spigot full on his head and savored the cool spray. He filled the sink and soaked his head, coming up for air and plunging down again when Spiro started preaching.

Beneath the water, he heard his dead mother's voice.

"When you were a baby, you drank from a bottle, got sick and messed your pants...and still you drink from a bottle and mess your pants..."

George came up shaking like a dog.

"You stink," said Spiro, dumping a bucket of trash from George's party into a barrel near the back door, a cascade of stale beer, soiled panties, busted condoms, and chewed food.

Deserting George, he said: "You talk dirty and you stink."

George opened the hot faucet on a bathtub against the wall, diarrhea running down the back of his legs and into his shoes. He lowered himself and lay his head back, water spilling over the side as he tried to sink below his problems.

No one gave a fuck.

He'd said so himself.

The sun pushed through block glass above George's head, dappling his body as though he had a skin disease, a leper bathing in sewage.

Getting out, dripping puddles as he looked for his clothes, George buttoned a soiled shirt over his wet chest and forced trousers over soaked shoes, tearing out the cuffs.

Holding onto the walls, he made his way behind the bar, palmed a pint of vodka and filled an empty pitcher with cold water. Walking back to the mop room, he edged around the trash barrel and stumbled out back to meet the day.

George's son Jimmy was dead almost three years now, killed and buried at Normandy. At thirty-nine, Leini suspected she was pregnant again but refused to believe it, unsure whose child it was because her husband often took her by force.

George squeezed into a thin shadow under the eaves, his back scraping against the bricks as he slid down with the pitcher. The sun had turned the alley into a field of broken mirrors and George cupped his eyes against its glare, squinting into tiny yards where women in black squirted down the concrete, heat bearing down through the oil in his hair.

But the sun could not penetrate his skull.

Not like George wanted.

It didn't melt his brain so the old ladies could squirt it into the sewer.

George pushed at his temples with his thumbs and unbuttoned his shirt, a golden Orthodox cross poking through the thick hair of his chest, glittering.

Turning his face to the sun, he mumbled a prayer no God would embrace: "Help me find them."

He tried to think of Leini with affection but saw instead the copper-assed girl who had bobbed before him a few hours ago, hands clasped behind her head.

Maybe the sun will bleach it all clean, he thought, like horse skulls in the desert.

Maybe Leini will lose her taste for pork.

I should just go home.

Muddy Waters was coming to Baltimore to sing the blues at a Greek nightclub in the basement of a Chinese laundry on the Fourth of July.

Anything was possible.

George took a sip of water from the pitcher and dribbled some on his chest, watching it disappear below tufts of hair, chilling the cross on his skin.

American flags hung from windows on both sides of the alley and smaller ones were tied to pepper plants and rosebushes. A gang of boys raced by on bicycles, honking tin horns; their bikes bright with crepe paper—blood red, pearl white, Hellenic blue—and noisy with playing cards clicking against the spokes.

George pried his eyes open as the kids ripped past; new Americans born to Old World wombs, little Jimmies flying by on tubes of Akron rubber and U.S. Steel.

The last boy—a dark-haired elf with black eyes, little Georgie just off the boat—waved.

"Mister George," the kid yelled. "Hey, Mister George..."

George brought the pitcher to his lips, took a sip, and dumped it on his head, rubbing the water into his aching neck. His hand slipped and the pitcher fell; banana-shards of glass gleaming like diamond-tipped sabers.

George stared at the broken glass for so long it changed colors, his eyes wandering down the alley when they started to hurt, settling on faded letters on the side of a building.

SHOE REPAIR!

SAVE MONEY!

BE SATISFIED!

"I can't be satisfied," George hummed.

I am in hell.

And no one is here but me.

He felt as alone as he did thirty years ago when he jumped ship, a twelve-year-old cabin boy in search of America, the country they said you could invent for yourself; determined not to be just another white-aproned Greek cracking eggs over a grill or standing on a ladder with a paintbrush in his hand.

Three decades later, anyone in East Baltimore could tell you that George Papageorgiou wasn't just another Greek. A real Greek always knows where his wife is.

George's people nearly killed themselves getting ahead in America and worked twice as hard to keep their children from succumbing to the culture that made prosperity possible.

After making their last mortgage payment, marrying their strong young Georges to their young virgin Leinis and living long enough to bounce little Jimmies on their knees, they were buried here.

The neighborhood was protective of young George at first, warning him to stay away from black people, easy money and strange birds like Spiro. They warned: "Find a good Greek girl before your America eats you up."

"I found her," said George, tickling his palm on the broken glass, pushing down until he punctured his skin.

Beyond the rooftops, distant sousaphones played "Stars and Stripes Forever," and, overcome with patriotism, George pulled out his bottle of vodka, cracked the seal and swallowed, the clear liquid seeping into his gums, pickling his tongue and firing gummed-up pistons in his head.

Dogs penned up in the small yards began running in tight circles, barking at a suitcase gray Mercury creeping through the alley, a sedan packed with guitars, drums, and five men from Chicago by way of the Great Magnolia State, their blood running back to a continent shaped like the head of a statesman.

Behind the wheel, the Big-Eye Beetle counted off doorways the way he counted out time before every song. Sitting shotgun, Muddy Waters squinted through the windshield, the Merc scraping the fence as it slowed alongside the Downbeat; his big, Oriental moon of a face quivering as he scolded the drummer for not parking around front.

"Safer 'round back boss. You know that."

Young, tough, and strong as an ox, Muddy glimpsed narrow concrete yards divided by rows of tomatoes and peppers, rosebushes and fig trees, but the only black faces he saw were the ones he'd brought.

He saw George Papageorgiou stagger to the gate.

"This the Downbeat?" asked the Beetle as a dozen screen doors opened to see what new trouble Spiro had imported.

George grabbed the gate post and nodded.

The drummer put the car in park and the band tumbled out, George stepping aside to let them pass as the radio predicted heavy humidity and holiday temperatures above ninety-five degrees.

Grabbing black cases held together with duct tape and cracked leather belts, the musicians made their way into the club, debating the chances of Eddie Arcaro aboard Citation back home at Arlington Park.

Bellowing welcome, Spiro rushed outside to greet Muddy, letting the band know that the Downbeat was good for all wagers.

Muddy nodded toward George and said: "Three to one that cat ain't standin' by showtime."

"Mr. Morganfield," said Spiro, reaching for Muddy's hand. "Mr. Morganfield, this is a great honor. Truly."

"Call me Muddy."

"Help these gentlemen set up," Spiro told George before disappearing into the club with his guest of honor. "Bring them whatever they need, some food, a cold drink. Anything."

George lugged in the Beetle's drum kit and tried to make conversation to keep from making trouble.

"Traveling long?"

"A hundred years," said the skinny drummer.

"Impossible."

"Goddamn impossible life."

Hauling the bass drum on his back, George noticed a sweet burning smell waft down from Spiro's office, like a coconut cake left in the oven too long. He stared up at the open window and pictured the scene: Good booze on the desk, a little sack of seasonings spread across yesterday's *Racing Form,* and Spiro waiting for the right moment to ask for a song.

Sure enough, music soon drifted down with the scent of smoldering hemp.

"Some nights she don't come home," sang Muddy. *"No peoples, sometimes she don't come home at all... the butcher, the baker, the wax-dick candlestick maker cry: 'Muddy Water, another mule be kickin' in your stall...'"*

George had never heard anything like it.

Creamy as a river bottom, it was not a salve.

Strange and compelling, it brought no comfort.

Deeper than the oceans, it doused nothing.

"All in my sleep, I hear my doorbell ring... Open the door for my baby, don't see a blessed thing. I be troubled, all worried in mind. If only I could hold you, could just be satisfied..."

George tapped the Beetle: "What's he talking about?"

"Somebody usin' what's his and don't belong to nobody else," the drummer laughed. "Tearin' it up, smoothin' it out."

"How do you find out if it's happening to you?"

"You don't know?"

"I know."

"So?"

"To be sure."

"You're not sure."

"Yes."

"You ain't?"

"I'm positive."

"So?"

"I want to know."

George stared at the window and saw Leini on her back, buried under a wagon of junk. Muddy's wail was making him thirsty.

"There's a way to find out," the drummer said. "Ain't hardly nobody knows the half of it."

"But you?" said George, offering his vodka.

"Course I know," said the Beetle, waving off the bottle and reaching into the Mercury for a canvas satchel. "Sure as I'm standing here."

The drummer flipped the keys to the bass player and told everyone to be back an hour before showtime. Watching the Mercury pull away, George knew that Leini could be anywhere.

Down in Tolchester or off in Ethiopia somewhere.

"Here," said the Beetle, passing George a bag of silk shirts: sunflower yellow and forest green, maroon guitars hanging on wild vines and Resurrection lilies damp with the sweat from one hundred years of a goddamn impossible life.

("I want to be an American, Mr. Spiro...")

("Come around on Sunday mornings and empty the trash for me, Georgie, I'll piece you off good, show you the ropes...the blues will wash the animosity from your heart.")

"My man," said the Beetle, sitting down on the steps. "Take my clothes to the laundry upstairs where a colored man can't go. Six shirts and two pair of slacks ready by showtime in exchange for one fool-proof rat trap."

"Just like that?"

"Shit yeah. I gotta get more for it than it cost me. And once you use it, it's yours to pass on for more than you paid...but remember, this ain't no pink pillow of Bayer."

"Excuse me?"

"It's spot remover."

"Okay," said George.

"Okay," said the Beetle. "This is what you gotta do if you wanna make muddy water..."

The Downbeat faded behind George one sip at a time.

I am being led like a cow, he thought, trudging out of the neighborhood in soggy shoes, into the deserted Eastern Avenue shopping district on his way to the end of Clinton Street.

The Avenue was hot and empty, cloaked in a holiday stillness. George didn't even see an open bar.

A few blocks away in Patterson Park, kids raced wheelbarrows and George could hear snare drums and cheers as five hundred immigrants took the oath of citizenship in the annual "I Am An American" celebration. Tonight there would be fireworks.

Above George's head, the crystal hands of the Great Bolewicki Depression Clock bubbled with water dyed red and blue for the Fourth.

"It's not too late," the clock tolled. "It's Independence Day all down the line..."

Passing under a railroad trestle with HIGHLANDTOWN lettered across it, George took a shot from his vodka and moved out of the bridge's shadow, putting his hand over one eye as he held up the bottle to see what he had left.

"You're blue, man," the drummer had said. "You been drinkin' from that jug all day. That's your blue jug."

At Clinton Street, George turned south and headed for the water, down to a dead-end he used to visit before he and Leini were married.

His wedding reception had been held in a tent behind Ralph's Lunch and he returned a week later when Ralph's burned to the ground, no one but Leini noticing the junk collector brooding atop his House of Half-Truths across the street.

George reckoned that he had a pinky's worth of booze left, shoved the bottle in his pocket and kept moving.

"Fucking witch doctors," he spat. "A man would just shoot them both."

A mile-and-a-half away, Spiro begged Muddy Waters to make his guitar sound like a cat being skinned alive.

In a white shingled house on an island near the mouth of the Chesapeake Bay, Orlo fluffed Leini's pillow and asked if she had ever tasted pasta dyed black with squid ink.

And alone in a corner of the Downbeat, the Beetle nibbled a salami sandwich and sipped a tall glass of beer, his drum kit on a plywood stage below a mural of a Greek fishing village.

The drummer ate with contentment, wondering what it was, precisely, that made it so thrilling to make-up stories.

People love lies, he decided.

They need them like they need air.

Like George Papageorgiou, with half of Clinton Street behind him and half yet to go, needed a shot of alcohol every twenty minutes to keep from seeing things.

The flame burning atop the Standard Oil refinery burned straight into the nickel haze, no breeze to push it around; oil tanks squatted shoulder-to-shoulder on the left, the brown harbor on George's right as heat rose from asphalt that led the way.

A cat slipped under a chain-link fence at a trucking company; Clinton Street was filthy with cats in the summer. They froze to death in the winter.

"A pussy cat," the Beetle had said. "No roosters."

George was getting dizzy watching cats dart from one side of the street to the other, stumbling forward for one ready to lose its whiskers when he noticed that Scheufel's was open.

The ginmill was empty except for a third-generation barmaid named Girlie and a pet monkey hanging from the water pipes in a beanie embroidered with the name "Dinky."

Dinky had been hanging at Scheufel's since a sailor on a South American run traded him even-up for a bar tab, back when Girlie was a girl. She'd taught Dinky to drink beer from a can and now they were growing old together.

George took a stool and pointed to the chimp.

"Gimme what he's having."

Girlie swept the hair back from her face, punctured a pair of triangles in a can of National Boh, and pushed it across the bar with a small, clean glass. George poured himself a drink and raised it to Dinky.

"George Papageorgiou," he said. "My pleasure."

Dinky screeched and swung down to the other end of the bar.

(George had warned Leini the last time, the time before that, and every time he wanted to knock her teeth out: "Don't you ever make a monkey out of me.")

He ordered another beer and went over the Beetle's formula in his mind.

Into his blue jug had to go the whiskers of a virgin cat, dirt from at least one back door where the deed was done (the Passover angel didn't have a list so long), something loved traded for something less, and no small part of himself.

"What kind of bullshit is this?" he had demanded.

"The kind you asked for," answered the drummer.

With his third beer, George took a silver dollar from his wallet that Spiro had given him on the day he became a citizen, held the coin in front of Girlie's face and said: "Yours."

"For what?"

"For nothing."

"Nothing's for nothin'."

"A trade."

"For what?"

"For nothing."

Girlie plucked a bobby pin from the thick hive swirling up from her forehead, leaned across the bar, and held it next to the dollar. George snatched the bobby pin as Girlie grabbed the coin.

"Okay, Girlie," he said, dropping the pin into his vodka bottle. "Okay for you."

The barmaid drew George a fourth beer from the cool box and told him it was on the house.

"God bless America," she said.

When the sun hit him, George realized he was drunk again.

"Goddamn," he said. "Goddamn crock of shit."

At Rhode's Shipyard he stopped to watch a billy goat chew weeds in a dusty lot and further down, the Lazaretto Point lighthouse stood dry and chalky alongside the boarded-up Home for Incurables, discarded by the city in a fit of post-war optimism.

At the copper docks, a white tugboat with *Athena* stenciled on her bow was lashed to an empty barge and where the asphalt stopped, all the way at the end, the red bricks and peaked slate roof of the Goose Hill branch of the Enoch Pratt Free Library stood next to the charred foundation that fewer and fewer people remembered as the ruins of Ralph's Lunch; the spot where Orlo had found Leini over a bowl of pig's feet in the summer of 1926.

Across Clinton Street, the decaying mansion of Leini's beloved—SALVAGE white-washed across its side in eight-foot high letters—loomed before the one she had never loved, waiting for George Papageorgiou to violate its secret portals.

The harbor sparkled like crinkled brown foil. George rubbed his eyes and kept going, the blue jug dragging down his pants in the back, exposing the crack of his ass to a sun well on the far side of noon.

At the seawall, a trash barrel overflowed with tuna cans and George remembered stories about the cat widows of Clinton Street, women without husbands—some who'd never seen a naked man—lonely do-gooders who fed strays and took kittens home before winter hit.

Leini knew the cat ladies well enough to say hello to, sometimes sparing a few nickels to buy milk for their darlings.

They blessed Leini for it, the only blessings that felt right to her since she'd begun to lay with Orlo, simple "God Bless Yous" offered as freely as if she had sneezed.

George shooed flies from the barrel and fished out a can, its edge orange with rust, wisps of fish stuck in the corners; nine cats poking out from the crumbling seawall to study him, ducking back when George leaned over the wall to fill the tin with water.

Sitting cross-legged in the street, George dipped his fingers in the can and flicked water on his face.

"Kitty, kitty," he purred. "Here, kitty, kitty..."

A white kitten walked out from behind a broken cinderblock, the others watching as she sniffed the tin between George's legs, whiskers like antennae as she drank.

When the water was gone, the kitten licked the flecks of fish as George scratched her neck.

"Yata...," he cooed, coaxing the baby into his arms. "Yatoula..."

The kitten stretched and licked the sides of her mouth as George cradled her against his shirt, rose to his feet, and with the force of pliers yanked the whiskers from the flesh alongside of her nose.

The cat squealed and lashed at George, catching him below the eye, claws digging deep into the drunkard's cheek, the pilfered whiskers sailing away with George's wailing curses.

Stumbling back, blood streaming down his face, George tightened his hand around the kitten's neck, sweat and tears needling his wounds, his screams bouncing off the corrugated walls of a warehouse on the docks.

"Fucking pussy cat!"

The Salvage House careened in and out of George's view as he twirled in pain—Leini on her back, Leini on her knees, Leini against the wall—his hands tighter and tighter around the cat's neck as the vodka stripped wax from Girlie's bobby pin; vapors of booze bathing the kitten's head as George waltzed with her, the cat ripping the tip of his nose and biting his lip, blood leaking onto yellow teeth.

George growled and hurled the kitten at the warehouse, banging it against graffiti that said "Helen is a whore."

Neck snapped, she fell dead as George came back to life, his face burning as he panted in the road, feeling better than he'd had in years.

George took his time—a moment to wipe his face and pat the bottle in his pocket, a few more to watch the sun sparkle over downtown—and when he knelt down to the corpse its whiskers gave way like strings popping off a third-grader's violin.

He laughed and his wounds widened, blood dripping cherry from the stubble on his chin; cackling with the knowledge that the busted onions who charged five bucks to suck the horns off a middle-aged Greek with nothing to live for would charge ten to service the same man with scars on his face.

George pressed the jug to his jaw, bottling his blood with kitty whiskers that pierced the potion like raw silk from a luminous shawl; whiskers darting around Girlie's bobby pin like sperm.

The only ingredients left were back door dirt and a touch of fire.

George picked the cat up by the tail and swung it at his side, dragging his feet across Orlo's dead summer lawn the way Leini could not stop dragging her heart across Stars and Stripes folded into a neat triangle.

On Orlo's cluttered acre were crab traps stacked in the shade of a soaring Ailanthus tree and a circle of skeletal jalopies being ground to dust on the edge of a small grove of peach trees. From the front porch, a wooden pier buckled into the harbor.

Invigorated by the death of the cat, George was greedy to hurt something more than he had hurt himself, too stupid to know it was impossible.

At the back door, he dusted the top step with the edge of his palm, crumbling soot and grime into his vodka bottle; the dirt drifting down to the venom.

He tried to peer through the thick glass in the door but met his reflection instead, kicking an unlocked door that wouldn't budge, never thinking to try the knob.

Setting his bottle where it would catch the last rays of daylight—temperatures still above ninety with the dinner hour at hand—George pulled the laces from his shoes and hung the cat from Orlo's door.

"Salvage this," he said, slumping down; the cat swaying gently above George's head as its blood dripped into his hair. Stretching in his sleep, George swatted at flies buzzing his cuts and dreamt of sunlight in an empty room.

Alone in the room, a woman years removed from Leini's womb and the night Muddy Waters came to Baltimore sat on a bare wooden floor.

She looked like Leini.

Just like Leini.

Except that her eyes were too close together.

Or perhaps too far apart; a beauty fouled by the vengeance of a lunatic and fathered by insanity or love but not by both; the Retarded Princess of Clinton Street sitting half-a-bubble off plumb in an Abdicated Castle of Junk bequeathed to her upon the death of her last parent.

Her unborn life dependent upon the choices George would make right now.

It was dark when the back door fell open, waking George; his potion cooked and cool as a warm breeze blew across the fresh, yolky scabs on his face.

Back at the Downbeat, the biggest eyes in the blues banged out time on a cow bell; the drummer's thin back covered in fresh linen as he laid down the beat behind a book of tragedies tumbling from the jowls of Muddy Waters.

"I be troubled, all troubled in mind," Muddy howled as George stumbled into the Salvage House. *"Cain't tell lies from the truth, just cain't be satisfied..."*

Waving his jug like a man shaking off advice that only makes him mad, George steadied himself on the kitchen table, feeling his way in the dark; a milky glow across the varnished table top from starlight pouring in through the back door.

Setting his bottle on the table, George recognized Orlo's Fedora hanging on a nail and spied a bottle of cooking wine on the stove. He put on the junkman's hat and grabbed the bottle, tossing the cork into the front room and sucking down the wine.

Circling the table, he stopped before the gleaming enamel of a new refrigerator, a big, upright slab of humming white metal with a wide, smooth door.

George grabbed a chair and sat before it, the only thing Orlo had ever bought new for himself, a luxury that kept meat fresh for days.

Even Spiro didn't have an electric ice-box at home.

Considering his reflection in the polished door, George admired the perfect fit of his cuckold's chapeau before jerking his head to free himself of it. As the hat hit the floor, he kicked it into the front room, the face in the fridge traumatized enough to be his own.

It spoke to him: "No one will tell you, George, but I will. I have watched them for years...the filthiest part of the filthiest swine...week after week after week..."

George's elbow slipped off the table, cracking his funny bone, pain shooting up through his jaw as he knocked over the vodka bottle, a crack leaking the potion across the table.

George opened the refrigerator and artificial light filled the room; the box clean and empty except for a carafe of ice water capped with a whittled cork; a cold mist pouring out with the light, cold stinging George's nostrils and frosting the tips of his ears, soothing his wounds.

When George opened the door to the freezer, he found bundles packaged in white butcher's paper and dated in Leini's handwriting, an edible calendar of assignations.

Fondling them like a blind man, George discovered that the packages weren't flat, like steaks or chops, nor were they curved like ribs.

Flush at one end, bumpy and almost square at the other, the meat felt like a cudgel.

George grabbed the meal for the coming week and kicked the door closed. Laying it on the table, he unwrapped the paper and smoothed it out with his fingertips.

"Feel like snappin' a razor in her face," sang Muddy. *"Let the boneyard be her restin' place..."*

Another fine evening at the Downbeat.

Everyone had a good time and no excuses were made for George, who pulled the paper out from under the pig's feet like a magician yanking a cloth from a table set for two.

With the edge of his fingernails, George rolled the trotters into the radiant ichor that had spilled.

Shaking the bobby pin from the bottle, George ran it across his teeth, tightening his lips around it before pushing it out with his tongue.

George used the pin to stab the pork over and over again before rubbing his poison into the holes; adulterating the delicacy with an invisible lover's litmus, guaranteeing for the rest of his miserable life not that he would be free or healed or reconciled or loved, but that every time people met the child to be born to Leini, they would wonder just what it was, precisely, that was so wrong with the girl.

Pinch the blossom . . .
sprinkle the nutmeg . . .

Red Cabbage and Apples

Pin-rays of sunlight bear down through black glass and dance in the dark circles under Leini's eyes, tiny beams of color crossing a face creased with despair.

Leini tilts her head back on a mahogany bench in the marble train station, the grand Acropolis of the Pennsylvania Line at Charles and Mount Royal in Baltimore.

She tries to rest—to be rested enough to recognize help if it appears—but she can not.

Leini opens her eyes and stares at a dome of stained glass, all twenty-three diametrical feet of its cathedral brilliance dead beneath black tar; dead like Leini except for thin rays of high noon pushing down through chips in the skylight's ebony coat.

Rainbow glass tarred a dozen years ago to give the Axis one less target.

Almost ten years the war's over, ten years my Jimmy is gone, mulls Leini, not sure if the dark glass is an agitation or a comfort. "Ten years, still black.

Orlo sits four rows behind his lover, watching splinters of light move yellow and red across a face he has kissed for nearly thirty years; green and blue tracing a mouth that hasn't smiled in ten.

They are waiting for the 2:12 Oriole Wing to New York City; off to see a specialist Orlo found in yellowed newsprint folded inside nursery rhymes tossed out with a pile of trash on Caroline Street.

"HERB DOCTOR OF CHINATOWN DELIVERS MIRACLE CURES."

Orlo went to Leini's first sanctuary, the Goose Hill branch of the

Enoch Pratt Free Library and found Yang among a thousand Yangs in a Manhattan phone directory.

The next morning, a letter sailed from the junkman's Salvage House to a healing room on Mott Street. Two weeks later, an answer arrived in small script: "Will try."

Orlo walked Leini to the end of the pier jutting out from his front lawn toward Fort McHenry, handed her a fresh peach from the small grove behind his house and made the pitch.

"Okay," she said. "Give me a couple days to figure out what to tell George."

Later, on a stifling Saturday morning in August of 1956, Leini left her husband at the kitchen table with a glass of ouzo and his hair in knots; Orlo hung a "CLOSED" sign in the window of the Salvage House and the Oriole Wing waited for all to board.

They met a few years before the Great Depression, sparks flying over bowls of pig's feet in a workingman's lunch room down at the end of Clinton Street.

Leini was seventeen, virgin and Greek.

Orlo would never be any of those things.

From that September day in 1926, the junkman and his teenage pony-tail nurtured a secret love forbidden by family, society, and the Greek Orthodox Church on Ponca Street.

I knew you first, she'd tell Orlo on his bad days, no need to say that she loved him first because there would never be a second.

"They picked my life," she said on the eve of her wedding, severing her heart from a Greek bridle to ally it with a blue-eyed American who roamed Baltimore in search of treasure. "But I chose you."

Thisavros.

Orlo picked up languages as easily as he found statues of St. Joseph buried in front yards; Polish, Italian, and Yiddish from his friends and customers; Greek from the torrents that came when Leini was excited, afraid, or angry.

Evrika to thisavro vois mou.

One week Orlo cooked, the next week Leini; back and forth in a delicious game of catch stretching across the century. The chef's trick was to outdo the last effort. The guest was expected to play along.

It was fun in the beginning, the Salvage House a Hollywood wardrobe for dress-ups as Orlo and Leini arrived at odd hours from different directions to meet for an hour or two, ferrying kettles of pig's feet into the woods behind the bottlecap factory; making campfires on the beaches at the end of Turkey Point Road, Bethlehem Steel vibrating in the distance, the aroma of slow-cooked pork wafting on the stench of molten steel.

"Look!" Orlo would say, pointing across the Patapsco to the tin mill. "The Parthenon!"

They rendezvoused in a suite of rooms at the top of the Bromo Seltzer Tower, the office of a big-shot who traded Orlo the use of a small kitchen and large sofa in exchange for the first shot at the week's harvest.

On and on it went, discreet messengers bringing maps showing the way to the next assignation.

Which years ago meant Smith Island, today means a marble train station on Charles Street, and in hindsight will seem no more exotic than a dog chasing its tail.

Getting up to stretch his legs, Orlo looks at Leini across the length of Penn Station and remembers the last time she cooked with enthusiasm, the last time she wanted to play. Before Jimmy had been killed.

She'd told him to dress like a chef and bring canvas pastry tubes of icing; told him to leave the pony home and meet her in an orange brick rowhouse a few blocks from her own in the 600 block of South Macon Street.

Orlo climbed the white marble steps and heard Satchmo blowing through the open slats of the jalousie. Leini met him at the door, snatching the tall white hat from his head and taking his hand, reminding him to bring the icing.

Climbing the stairs behind his lover, Orlo glimpsed a saloon table in the parlor set with Limoges, linen, and silver; a table set for two; the house cool and empty except for Orlo and Leini and a cauldron of pig's feet simmering in pearl onions and peppercorns.

In another couple's bed at the front of the house, they took turns reading newspaper crime stories to one another—"Jealous Roland Park husband drowns wife in tub of dirty laundry..."—and made love beneath a statue of Saint Lucy holding her eyes on a platter like hors d'oeuvres.

On each side of Lucy were framed photographs of someone else's family: stern husband, a wife without expression, and three smiling children looking down on Orlo and Leini as sunlight sparkling through venetian blinds cast stripes across their skin.

"Thank you," murmured Leini. "Thank you for loving me."

Leini wears her habit today, her best disguise ever, the one that makes her invisible, that she will not surrender: mourning dress from shawl to shoes, just another dried fig in black with swollen ankles and a bad heart.

Orlo walks in wide circles around the station, moving closer on each pass, watching Leini take a novel from her canvas bag, open it and pull an envelope that has marked her place in every book she has read since the war ended.

From the envelope, she slips a letter that has endured a thousand foldings. On wisps of pulp, it survives another.

Orlo reads his lover's lips as his lover reads the letter, mouthing its content in unison with her like a bored priest at weekday Mass.

"Dear Ma, it's almost over and I'm almost home. I found a swell recipe for pig's feet in an old bookstore over here (enclosed), maybe one you don't know. A nice girl translated it for me. She's real cute, Ma, wait'll you meet her. I know you won't mind that she's not Greek. I'll deal with Dad.

"It calls for vinegar and nutmeg and you serve it with red cabbage and roasted apples. Enjoy it with your friend and think of me. Be happy now, Mama. I'm coming home."

Leini rubs the envelope against her cheek.

"Love, Jimmy."

Orlo makes himself breathe, tips back his hat, and walks to his bench, remembering what Leini had told him over the phone on her kitchen wall the day Jimmy's letter arrived from France.

"Orlo, he knows. He knows and it's okay. Red cabbage and apples! Orlo! Maybe it's time...when Jimmy comes home..."

Later that day, Leini showed up at the junkman's door.

"My Jimmy's dead," she cried, holding a telegram from the United States of America like a handkerchief. "He knew and he's dead."

Leini took her son's death as a consequence.

Is it not our choices which determine how bruised the velvet?

The flavor of the game forever changed as she went down with her grief.

"ALL ABOARD THE PENNSY LINE, 2:12 ORIOLE WING TO WILMINGTON, 30TH STREET PHILADELPHIA, NEWARK, AND THE LAND OF MANHATTOES BELTED ROUND BY WHARVES..."

Leini boards the train five cars up from Orlo and takes a seat in a chair car, a floating living room of worn furniture and stained carpet in the golden age of the automobile.

She stares out the window as the train pulls away and wonders what a nut doctor named Yang can possibly tell her that she doesn't already know; a slow click and roll taking her away from a black skylight on a hot Saturday in July.

Orlo sits in a smoking car an eighth-of-a-mile behind Leini, waiting to light a cigar, watching as the platform gives way to freight yards and the blur of downtown as the Oriole Wing gathers speed.

All this trouble, he thinks; nothing but trouble and even now, on a fast train out of town, she will not let me sit beside her in public.

I am fifty-eight years old, an old man getting older without children or grandchildren to help pull my wagon. We should just keep going. Listen to what this guy has to say and keep going.

Brave talk from a man who had turned down the same offer from his lover so many times that she buried the idea alongside her soldier boy.

Orlo wonders if they'll get the chance to share a bowl of pig's feet in New York and his mouth waters for Leini on a velvet bedspread.

He wants to race through the train and scream in her face: You never baked the apples!

You and your friend enjoy, that's what the letter said.

Sprinkle the nutmeg.

On her best days, Leini manages a boiled potato on the side; this from a woman who once boned six pig's feet and marinated them for a week before stuffing the meat with spinach, bread crumbs, garlic, and mushroom, all under her husband's nose.

Now—in the modern world of color television and rights for the colored, rocket ships and rock and roll—Orlo and Leini sit in separate cars on a northbound train to see a Chinaman who heals with herbs.

Orlo lights his cigar and allows the match to burn his thumb.

"A goddamn witch doctor," he mutters.

Ribbons of purple silk studded with gems.

Strings of seashells.

And pajama buttons carved from hard woods.

The curtain parts upon the brow of a young boy.

"Dr. Yang will see you now."

Orlo helps Leini out of her chair and they step across the threshold into Yang's eight-sided examining room.

"Mr. Junkman," says Yang, shaking Orlo's hand.

"This is Leini," says Orlo.

The doctor bows, looks back and forth between the man and the woman before him and finds sad and sadder, no way and maybe, too late and just in time.

He knows he cannot help them both, but that is not what people come to hear.

"Why need Yang?"

Orlo hesitates. They'll never get what they need if he lets Leini tell it, but before he can explain, she spills more words than she has spoken in a year.

"It hurts...locked up the whole time I was growing up, everywhere I went somebody watching and waiting to tell where they saw me and what I'd been doing...Orlo showed me how to be invisible and we went anywhere we wanted and it was so much fun I wanted it all the time. All the time for a long time. And then they killed my Jimmy and I was back in the old place, all the way back after all those years and I can't find my way out..."

Leini bites her lip and forces her wedding ring over the dry knuckles of her thumb, pushing it up and down until it bleeds. Yang paces, a finger to his lips.

"Mr. Junkman," he commands. "Go down to street. At end of block turn right. Down to middle of next block is alley. Alley take you to butcher on sidewalk. Can't miss: carcass hang from bamboo—pig, goose, lamb. There find Tim, butcher. Buy feet of one sow, not too old. Tell Tim—want pig more young than old. Four feet. Boy will wait. Go."

Orlo looks at Leini and then at Yang. Halfway through the brilliant curtain, he turns to ask a question that has simmered in his gut for thirty years.

"What do I get out of it?"

"Dinner!" roars Yang and Orlo stumbles away like a man who's been beaten across the shoulders.

Alone with Leini, the Chinaman ranges between high shelves and glass cabinets, pinching stems and blossoms and piling them together with petals and roots on a chopping block in the middle of the room.

Yang gathers white rose buds, a giant rafflesia, and dogtooth violets and over them shreds a young Alanthus tree—no more than a big weed—before working the pile over with a sharp knife.

"Talk."

Leini slips a hand inside of her blouse and stares at her shoes.

"I told you, it hurts. Like my heart is tearing away from itself."

"Everything in head," says Yang, scraping the chopped flowers back to the middle of the block before going over them again. "Maybe coming, maybe going, but always in head."

"Why does it feel so good to tell lies?" asks Leini.

"Lie is cannibal," says Yang. "Never satisfied."

"It's my only happiness," says Leini.

Yang sprinkles something thick and yellow from an old Noxema bottle over the pile and breathes over the herbs until they are dry.

"That is why you come see Yang? Because you are happy?"

The question stabs Leini. She wants to cry.

"Help me."

"Help self," says Yang, crumbling his concoction into linen pouches and tying them with string used to truss fowl.

"I just hold on."

"Maybe should let go."

Seven blocks away, as Orlo dumbly watches a hag named Tim hack at the shins of a female pig, the Junkman of Clinton Street feels his intestines drop to his scrotum.

Yang hands three pouches of herbs to Leini, gently shows her the door, and calls his next patient.

Returning with bundles in white butcher's paper, Orlo meets Leini and the house boy outside of Yang's office. The junkman tries to give the meat to the boy but the kid pushes it away; leading the lovers down a hallway to a small kitchen.

At the door, the boy points to the pig's feet, the herbs, and the stove.

"Her turn, yes?"

"Yes," says Leini and the boy disappears.

On top of an enamel gas range sits a large aluminum pot. A pink Formica table set for two hugs a wall divided by a porthole that looks over the meat packing district of Chinatown.

Leini takes the pork from Orlo and unwraps it in the sink, the counter set up with sliced ginger, ingots of brown sugar, a bottle of black vinegar, and three large eggs.

Orlo roots through bins for the cursed head of cabbage.

"Did you tell Yang it was your turn?"

"No," says Leini, bringing the pouches to her nose, liking the scent so much that she moves her lips across them.

Tacked into stained plaster behind the stove is a thin strip of rice paper splattered with grease and marked in Yang's tiny script.

"Boil...drain...rinse...scrape...rinse...simmer...use all herbs...eat to fill..."

Leini follows Yang's recipe to the pinch, to the drop. Orlo struggles with small talk, trying to believe that one meal out of a thousand will make a difference, forgetting that the first one turned the world upside down, that any difference is all the difference.

Orlo comes up behind Leini and puts his arms around her waist as she lowers the eggs into the boiling water on a spoon. He tickles her, trying to add a dollop of laughter.

He teases: "You believe any of this?"

"You're going to make me break one of these," she scolds, prying his hands away to sprinkle the first pouch into the water, watching the herbs churn with the rolling eggs.

On a back burner, the vinegar bubbles in a shallow pan. In it, Leini dissolves the brown sugar and a second pouch of herbs. Orlo feels a rush of optimism and kisses her on the neck.

"Let's get through the meal," she says.

When the pig's feet are ready, Leini takes them from the pot, drains the trotters on a sideboard and slices meat from the knuckles, arranging slivers of pork on a pale ceramic dish.

She cracks the soft-boiled eggs and scoops their goo over the pork, pouring the vinegar and brown sugar sauce into a gravy boat shaped like a Chinese junk.

Leini sprinkles the contents of Yang's last pouch over the entire meal and tosses her apron on the sink.

"It's ready," she says, bringing the food to the table and sitting down.

"Ready or not," says Orlo.

They eat for nearly an hour, slow and steady without talking, waiting for the roof to open up and the god of foolish decisions to come down and save them.

The meal is exquisite; sweet and vague and sour and familiar.

Like none before.

Yet they dine with effort, swallowing the meat like a sick kid choking down a horse pill. When the last piece is left, Orlo rinses his mouth with water and spears it.

Leini is aghast, looking at Orlo as if he has grabbed the last life preserver on a sinking ship. Shredding the pork with his teeth, Orlo gets up and moves around the table to Leini, swallowing half the meat and holding the rest in his cheek, pig fat and herbs seeping through the cracks in his gums, down to his jaw.

Too full to move, Leini sits mute as Orlo rewrites Yang's precise instructions. Straddling her, the junkman pins Leini in the chair and holds her wrists above her head.

Parting her lips with his own, he transfers the last of the pork to her mouth, pushing it to the back of her throat with his tongue; pushing until she swallows.

"Water," says Leini as Orlo licks sticky black sauce from her lips.

Orlo brings a glass to her mouth and Leini gulps the drink down. The glass falls when he tries to set it down, rolling to the edge of the table.

The junkman licks drops of water from the corners of his lover's mouth and with every bit of strength left to him at fifty-eight—old and getting older, no children or grandchildren to comfort him—he lifts her black dress, yanks her white cotton panties down to shoes only a nun would wear, and fucks her in the kitchen chair.

With each scrape of linoleum, Yang's herbs seep further into their blood and, as Orlo savors the best sex he has had in a decade, he wonders if the magic in his veins will reach his semen by the time his semen reaches Leini.

Orlo spins inside of her like a wheel, shooting a constellation of small, bright stars across a long arc shaped like a serving spoon; hoping, as he comes, that a forty-six-year-old woman in the vestibule of menopause will conceive a tableside miracle in Chinatown.

"Don't stop," moans Leini, lifting a leg to the table.

Orlo works until his beloved joins him on the other side and they hold one another; declaring in gasps and whispers how much they love each other.

Up or down.

Pig's feet or porridge.

Pulling back, they look for clues in each other's eyes but only see their own reflections.

Orlo climbs off of Leini and walks to the sink, cupping water in his hands and splashing his face. Leini uses a napkin to wipe her thighs, tosses it on the table and heaves up her drawers.

As Orlo follows her out of the room, he snatches the recipe from the nail in the wall and shoves it in his pocket. They ask to see Yang on their way out but are refused.

"Yang done," says the boy, handing Orlo the bill: Eleven dollars and a promise to abide, always, to Leini's wishes, however rough that might be.

Orlo pays the bill and tips the kid a buck while Leini runs her fingers over the baubles on the purple ribbon between her and the examining room. Brushing her sex-flushed face against the curtain, Leini hears a woman tell Yang how bad it hurts but cannot discern the doctor's response.

The Oriole Wing glides south to Baltimore; the marble railway hall quiet and empty, black night filling chips in paint that silence a rainbow.

Orlo stares out the window at the city of his birth, a passing blur of white marble and orange brick.

Tarred rooftops zip by like black hats sewn together at their brims, each one adorned with a small brick chimney in the shape of an A; rowhouse after rowhouse of families asleep with secrets of their own as the Holy Land passes in the moonlight.

People who can't sleep sit on the sidewalk in folding chairs, catching a breeze in the night, sipping something cold and making conversation as Orlo sits next to Leini in a deserted rail car.

In one of the houses is Leini's husband, their seven-year-old daughter, and a framed picture of Jimmy in uniform alongside the single bed where Leini will sleep tonight.

Orlo fingers Yang's receipt and wonders how he could possibly surrender anymore than he already has to the crumbling beauty at his side.

Where does our time go?

All those years ago in a lunch room down at the end of Clinton Street.

Long enough for Orlo to find a small fortune in the debris of other people's lives; to bury two horses, stuff a third, and wear out a heavy truck; time enough to build a library with more recipes for the meat above the hooves of swine than the French have sauce for fish.

And now he has another, a story to go with it, and traces of magic herbs beneath his fingernails.

With the light of the station upon them, Orlo turns to look at Leini, her eyes closed, an open book in her lap.

"I love you little girl," he says, touching her bare arm.

Leini wakes and kisses the junkman on the cheek, giving him a gentle nudge as the train begins to slow.

"Better get back to your seat," she says. "We're home."

Layers of pork upon
layers of salt upon
layers of pork . . .

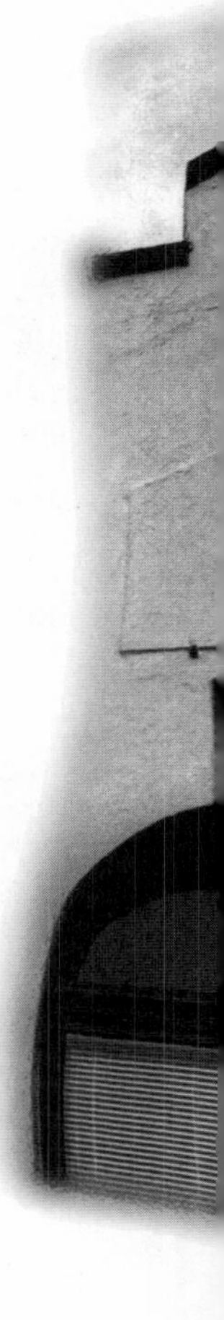

Christmas Eve

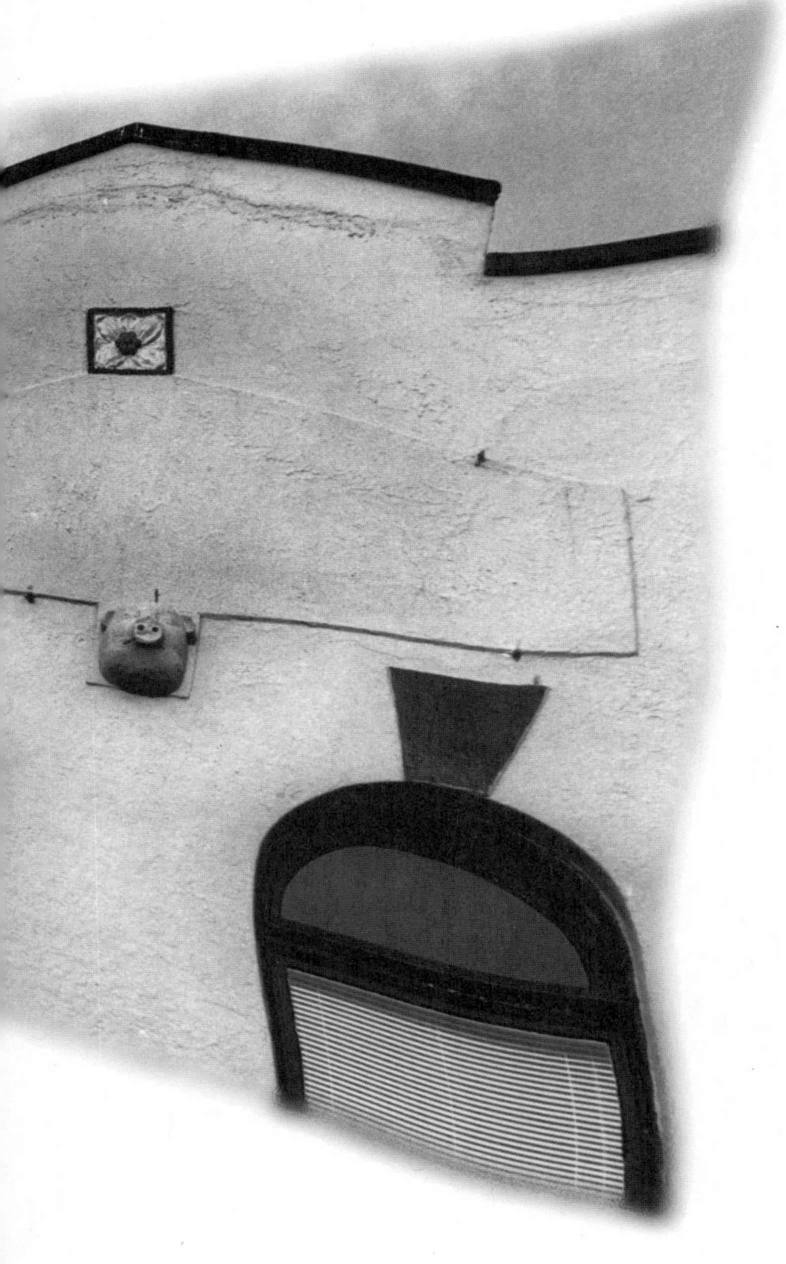

Wigmann came to a few hours before dawn on Christmas Eve, face down on the sofa of a rowhouse saloon in the Holy Land. The old beer garden had been in his family since the turn-of-the-century and passed down to him with the recent death of his father.

Wigmann rubbed the back of his neck.

"What am I going to do, Pop?"

The photograph stared back at him, mute alongside a bowl of ginger snaps soaking in sweet vinegar on the bar. The woman who'd promised to transform the cookies into sour rabbit and dumplings—a girl named Barbara he would introduce to the family tonight at dinner, the one who'd grown weary of apology—should have arrived hours ago.

A toy train emerged from a tunnel behind the wall with a shrill whistle and bubble lights percolated against the silvery sheen of a tin ceiling, reflecting in mirrors advertising "The Land of Pleasant Living," the destination Wigmann had sought while waiting for his sweetheart.

She'd many miles to cover and Wigmann had bided his time with one more beer.

Just one more.

Standing, he killed the train and walked to the front door, a draft frosting his toes as he turned the locks, the door bumping against something heavy.

Slipping outside, feet freezing against tiles that spelled out "645 Newkirk Street," Wigmann beheld a heart-breaking bounty.

A pile of presents, ribbons fluttering in the wind, were arranged around a roasting pan. Bending to lift the lid, Wigmann set his fingertips against the frozen skin of a cooked goose and began mourning the loss of his private Christmas: a German chapel crumbling inside an Italian cathedral.

Wigmann rifled through the gifts, but his beloved—who'd banged on the door with the heel of her shoe and let the phone ring a hundred times—had not left a note.

Tradition, Basilio's grandfather often said, is nothing more than hard work and planning.

The calendar is not a line, but a loop, and you could not trust something as important as tradition—Christmas Eve the richest of all—to chance.

As Wigmann wept into his pillow, Basilio's grandfather stood at a basement workbench alongside a stone tub where eel would soon soak in milk.

The Spaniard was hammering together a gift for his namesake grandson, an easel made from grape crates.

(The wine had turned out especially good that year, fruity and crude, the white better than the red and the words "Boullosa & Sons" written across clay jugs before gifts of it were made to friends and relatives who lived along the alley that separated Macon Street from Newkirk; an extra bottle delivered to Wigmann's Beer Garden to help ease the loss there. As sad as it was, the dead man's son was supposed to bring a new face to the table and in this way, girded by hard work and new blood, tradition rolled with the calendar.)

Driving the last screw and oiling the hinges, Basilio's grandfather brought the easel from the back of the basement into the long kitchen where the feast would take place, where his Italian wife sat separating anchovies to be deep fried in dough.

"It's finished Mom," he said.

Weak-sighted, the woman wiped her hands on her apron and used her fingertips to make out the easel's form beneath a ring of fluorescent light on the ceiling.

"It's good."

"I think so," said Grandpop, putting away his tools.

Two floors above, Little Basilio slept with dreams coursing through his brain in the shape of his age: a pair of perfect circles, one set atop the other.

Inside the endless eight, the boy raced through the games he would play that night, felt the long wait ahead and realized why he was born.

(Born to paint the pictures in his head, to sketch the kitchen in the basement, to capture the clouds as the wind drove them past the bottle cap factory down by the railroad tracks, to capture the air that swirled across the tarred rooftops.)

The night before, Basilio had gone to bed knowing that he liked to draw.

Today, he would wake up with the knowledge that he was an artist the way his father was a tugboat man and his grandfather was a machinist down at the shipyard.

A skylight above Basilio's head—hexagon panes embedded with diamonds of twisted wire—brought the breaking day into his room on a rolling bank of low, nickel-gray clouds, the kind that tease children with the promise of snow.

The boy opened his eyes and, inside the skylight glass, he saw himself as a grown man living with his aged grandfather, painting the day-by-day story of their life together.

Basilio's father—at home with the rest of his family on a cul de sac where no one baked eel for Christmas—had slept below the same skylight thirty years before and told the boy over and over of the sacrifices made for a better life among the lawns outside the city.

Yet every weekend, summer vacation, and Christmas Eve, Basilio's parents dropped him off on Macon Street.

To walk to the corner for wheels of fresh bread.

Wake up to the scent of smelts frying in olive oil.

And measure the universe by the width of a narrow rowhouse in the Holy Land.

Basilio heard his grandfather's feet coming up the stairs and knew it was time to go to the fish market.

Today was the day.

Wigmann took the gifts that had been left on his doorstep and packed them in his old man's car. He piled the packages on the back seat and set the roasting pan on the floor, thinking, as he walked back and forth between the house and the car, of the Christmas Eves of his childhood.

There was no place for goose at his family's feast. The tables pushed together in the basement of his aunt's house down the alley would be crowded with thirteen kinds of seafood in honor of the Savior of the World and the twelve who had followed Him.

Every year, Wigmann's father would lead all of the children from the crowded table to the beer garden to watch trains run through a sawdust village of nineteenth century Germany.

With the big meal a dozen hours away—his father dead and his sweetheart gone—Wigmann wasn't sure if he could stomach it this year.

The singing. The hugs. The love.

A basement filled with his mother's family: the bombastic Bombaccis.

Seeing a light on in his Aunt Lola's house across the alley, Wigmann plucked a present from the pile, let himself into her small backyard, and knocked on the kitchen door.

Wigmann's mother and Lola were the youngest and oldest of five first-generation sisters who lived up and down the alley.

Tonight's feast would take place in the middle of the block, at the home of Francesca Boullosa, the middle sister and grandmother of an eight-year-old boy who had just awoken with the knowledge that he was born to paint everything he saw.

Tapping lightly against the glass until Lola pulled the curtains, Wigmann held the gift to the window as his aunt squinted, looking tired and confused. As his aunt opened the door, Wigmann realized that he hadn't been a boy for a long time.

A combination of his father's mind and his mother's heart—his mother's dark eyes and his father's straight jaw—Wigmann often wanted to cry, but seldom did.

"Merry Christmas, Aunt Lol. It's me."

"You're up early, hon," said Lola. "Want some coffee?"

"No thanks. I just wanted to give you a little something in case I don't see you tonight."

"Not see me?" said Lola, taking the gift.

"Open it," said Wigmann, wondering what he'd given her.

"I'll put it under the tree."

Wigmann looked around the spotless rowhouse.

"Aunt Lol," he said. "You don't have a tree."

"Here," said Lola, pushing a hot cup of coffee on him with a thin Italian waffle cookie. "Take something with you. It's cold outside."

Basilio gathered nickels and dimes and quarters from the bedroom dresser, slipped them into his pockets with a handful of colored pencils, and ran downstairs.

Next to the Basilio's place at the table—years later, the artist would stand in the basement and recite his family's seating arrangement for visitors—stood an easel he would use long after the sidewalks had cracked on Macon Street.

"Sit," said his grandmother, touching the back of the boy's head, a plate of buttered toast and bowl of Cream of Wheat waiting for him.

"When can I try it?" he asked.

"Eat," said Grandpop. "Then wash up."

In the car, as Basilio drew on the inside of the windows with his fingertips, Grandpop told the boy why the day was so special: "So you won't forget. The empanada, my mother made it with chopped nuts. Your grandmother uses raisins. One day, if you marry the right girl, she will make it and I'll be gone."

"You're funny, Grandpop."

Together, the pair walked through the aisles of Broadway Market, and, as Basilio strained to see what was in the window of a record store across the street, Grandpop pulled him toward the crushed ice of the fish stalls—do this in memory of me spiced with five pounds of shrimp—and repeated why this day was important.

But Basilio was thinking the thoughts of an eight-year-old who wakes up one day with the knowledge of his existence: of listening to Beatles' records with his cousin Donna and which new albums they might receive; of how long would it be before she walked through the front door of their grandparents' house with her red plastic record player and what would happen, just what he wondered, if he tried to kiss her during a slow song.

"Today, we eat like kings," said Grandpop.

(Anyone blessed to eat their fill wore a crown. Enough potatoes. Orchards of fruit. And a sea of fish across three tables pushed together and covered with white cloth.)

The black eel—his wife's tradition, Bombacci and Boullosa mixed together in his restless grandson like pigments on a palette—was a once a year treat: its sweet, firm length divided by the inch, breaded, baked, and served on pastel china.

"You nail the head to a piece of wood and pull the skin back with pliers because she is too slippery to hold," said Grandpop as the fish man coiled three feet of eel into the bottom of a sack.

Basilio reached out and touched the creature just before it disappeared.

"Grandpop," said Basilio, "can we stop at the record store on the way home?"

Wigmann sped east on Eastern Avenue with Aunt Lola's coffee at his lips and the roasted goose rocking gently near his feet.

Seeking absolution—the God of Second Chances was here Wigmann, right here in the Holy Land while you were passed out—he turned south onto Clinton Street and raised a cold cloud of dust, rumbling toward the water's edge, praying that a third chance would be the charm, a fat wad of inherited cash in his pocket.

Halfway down the gravel road, the mansion at the old Pound shipworks rose before Wigmann, higher than the tongue of flame above the Standard Oil refinery, an ornate, nineteenth century structure: the Salvage House.

It looked worse for wear against the nickel-gray sky as Wigmann pulled into the yard; the gutters sagging, paint peeling from the upper floors, and a quartet of gargoyle pigs sneering down from the building's roof.

Wigmann got out of the car with the roasting pan, drawing the attention of a gray-haired man slashing the thick skin of pig's feet with an oyster knife, scoring the trotters before tossing them into a black kettle over a backyard fire.

Orlo Pound was pickling enough Christmas pig's feet to give to all the people who'd helped keep his secret, enough left over to share with his lover. He tended the pot in a small circle of bare peach trees at the edge of the Patapsco on a cold morning in late December; chuckling as he stirred with a broom handle, a trio of Retrievers trying to stick their snouts in the bubbling vat, an empty cask waiting to receive layers of pork upon layers of kosher salt and onions and spice upon layers of pork.

Wigmann remembered coming down to the Salvage House with his father when he was a kid; how Orlo would give him gadgets from his great store: pocket watches without hands and port holes without glass that a kid could stick their head through and pretend to be at sea.

So many more thoughts of his old man in death than before.

Remembering, remembering, remembering.

Christmas...the time for remembering a wind-up toy the junkman called a "Dinky Doll," a monkey that hung from pipes on the ceiling while raising a tiny can of beer to his lips; remembering how he'd lost Dinky before he could show it to anybody and how hard, being a big boy of eight or nine, he'd tried not to cry in front of his father.

Back when Orlo had nothing but youth and conflict and yearning in his life—wanting Leini to be his and his alone, not caring to share her with her children much less her husband—back when the junkman kept the mansion in perfect shape.

Now he was too content to get up on a ladder.

Laying the churning stick aside as Wigmann approached, Orlo let out a belly laugh that smothered the sad and beautiful world of pain he'd survived, recognizing in the disappointed face of the saloon keeper's son the little boy he used to know.

"Junior!" cried the junkman. "I thought that was you."

And in that moment—the boy gone from a man who looked nothing like his father—Orlo remembered that young Wigmann was the nephew of his lover's best friend.

Francesca Bombacci Boullosa and Eleini Leftafkis Papageorgiou had been close as sisters since attending P.S. 228 together on Rappolla Street.

When the pretty girl from Greece enrolled in the fourth grade without knowing five words of English, the feeble-sighted Francesca helped with her homework and invited her to family dinners in houses along the alley separating Macon and Newkirk streets.

All these years later, Francesca remained the newly widowed woman's best friend.

"Hi Mr. Orlo," said Wigmann, taking a seat in a metal folding chair near the fire, freezing his ass off as the junkman par-boiled a cauldron of trotters.

"What brings you down here after all these years? Doing some last minute Christmas shopping like your old man used to do?"

Once Wigmann hit puberty, he didn't want to hang out too often with his father or tag along on the annual holiday visit to the Salvage House for last minute gifts you couldn't get in stores.

One Christmas Eve, Wigmann told his father he didn't feel like going to Mr. Orlo's, the same way he told himself this dawn—staring down at a pile of gifts on his freezing stoop—that he didn't want to wait for Jesus to be born in his Aunt Francie's basement on Macon Street anymore.

The next year, the boy begged off again and after that his old man didn't ask his son to go anywhere with him anymore.

"Dad's gone," said Wigmann, taking the lid from the roasting pan and ripping off a leg from the goose, the dogs jumping on his lap.

"I know, I was at his funeral."

"How old are you now, Mr. Orlo?"

"Sixty-seven last summer."

"Dad was only fifty-two," said Wigmann, pushing aside the lid to the roasting pan and tearing off a drum stick, gnawing on it as he picked meat from the carcass and threw it to the dogs. "It's our first Christmas without him."

The bird was delicious. Chewing slowly, watching the dogs fight for scraps, Wigmann wondered how the meal would have tasted warm from the oven with Barbara, a white cloth spread across the bar. He threw the dogs a bone and started on a wing.

"Save me the wishbone," said Orlo.

"What's your wish?"

"I'm saving enough to build a star."

Wigmann pointed to the kettle.

"What's that?"

"Holiday ritual," said Orlo. "Pickled pig's feet with fig jam."

"For you and your friend? She used to give us Hershey bars wrapped in red and green cellophane when we were little. She still gives them to the little kids wrapped in five dollar bills."

"How can I help you, Junior?"

Wigmann lifted the goose from the pan like a football and tossed it into the middle of the yard, watching as the dogs ripped the bird to shreds and ground its bones to paste.

"I need an engagement ring."

"Ah," said Orlo, covering the pot. "We've got plenty of those."

Inside the house, Orlo's kitchen looked exactly the same to Wigmann as it did when he was little and his father and the junkman would eat bowls of pig knuckles with spaetzle, washing it down with glass pitchers of beer.

Orlo moved toward a stove near the hallway, fiddling with the knobs on the oven as Wigmann inspected a china cabinet filled with records and buttons and school lunch boxes adorned with the faces of three young men with long hair and guitars and one goofy looking guy with long hair and a drum set.

"What's this?" he asked, tapping the cabinet glass.

Orlo turned the oven knob 350 degrees to the left, char-broil to the right, and 200 degrees to the left and the oven door popped open with a loud click.

"What's what?" said Orlo, pulling a tray of rings from the oven rack.

Wigmann tapped the glass again.

"What are you doing with this kiddie stuff?"

"I've always collected fun, Junior. You know that."

"But why this?"

"Because they're going to be huge and they make me smile," said Orlo. "This kid Frankie Lidinsky over near St. Wenceslaus gets everything the minute it hits the street and tells me what to look for."

"People are already throwing it away?"

"Not yet," said Orlo. "But there's a ton of it out there."

"What's that hairy thing?"

"Hair."

"Who's?"

"John's."

"The leader?"

"Yes."

"I don't believe it."

"So don't."

"Where'd you get it?"

"From a friend whose old lady makes up beds at the Holiday Inn. She worked their rooms when they were here in March. Already been offered a grand for it."

"Gimme Frankie and Dino," said Wigmann. "I can't stand all that screaming."

"Some of it is very nice," said Orlo, walking the rings to the kitchen table, the tray a chest of pirate's jewels, alive in the sunshine streaming through the window above the sink.

Wigmann picked up the rings one at a time, slipping them on all of his fingers as far as they would go—"Okay, Ringo!" laughed Orlo—and began separating them into piles: diamonds, emeralds, rubies, ornate antique settings and sleek modern ones; sapphires, opals, and pearls.

"There's no prices," said Wigmann.

Orlo brought a cutting board to the table and began mashing cloves and grinding allspice across from Wigmann; a large bowl of kosher salt waiting, the room scented with the fragrance of nutmeg and cinnamon as a pot of figs boiled on the stove.

"Let me tell you about your father."

Wigmann stopped playing with the rings and sat up.

"Your old man was quite the character," said Orlo. "He'd come down here on afternoons when he couldn't stand being behind that bar a moment longer."

I know that feeling, thought Wigmann.

"And of course he loved everything German. He *loved* that Babe Ruth was German. That Mencken was German. These great Americans from Baltimore. I'd open up my Germanica room, he'd put on lederhosen, and we'd drink beer out of steins shaped like Bavarian castles."

"Can I see the room?"

"It's all doorknobs now," said Orlo. "Floor to ceiling doorknobs. After he had a few, he'd get very serious and start talking about how he envied me because I was a real American, free, he said, absolutely free."

"He envied you?"

"Yes and no," said Orlo. "He envied how I could go anywhere at anytime for any reason without having to explain. Still could if my legs didn't ache so much. He envied my freedom and I envied him his son."

"Me?"

"Your father missed you coming down here with him. It upset him that you didn't want to come down here anymore."

"It's not that I didn't want to."

"It's the only time I saw him cry."

"Is that true?"

"You'll hear it said that people love lies," said Orlo. "I don't believe it."

"How come people hurt each other without meaning to?"

"I said I wouldn't lie to you, Junior. I didn't say I could split the atom. All I know about it is sitting on this table and out back in the pickling tub."

"But I thought..."

"Nope," said Orlo.

"I've been messing up," Wigmann said. "I was expecting my girl last night and instead I got drunk and missed her. We were going to have an old-fashioned German Christmas, candles on the tree, just the two of us."

"Every year somebody burns their house down trying to have an old-fashioned Christmas," said Orlo.

"This is the big night, *the* night you wait all year for," said Wigmann. "And there's nothing I want to do less than sit around that table."

(I'd like to be there, thought Orlo, chuck this swine and enjoy a nice plate of fish. Wouldn't I love to hold her hand next to a cup of coffee and a plate of Christmas cookies.)

"Why not?" asked Orlo. "Because your girl won't be there?"

"She might," said Wigmann, separating the rings into three piles: maybe, forget it, and gotta have it; his father's money tingling in his pocket as he played eenie-meenie-miney-mo with an emerald and a ruby. "There's nothing I was looking forward to more than her knock on the door. Did my Dad really say that stuff about me?"

"Come on Junior. You come down here for the first time in a dozen years to ask questions there ain't no answers to and then you don't believe what I tell you."

"I wish he'd have told me himself," said Wigmann. "I feel rotten because I miss Barbara more than I miss him."

"Of course you do," said Orlo.

"I want to chuck it all."

"I've ridden that train," laughed Orlo.

"You think it's funny?"

"Didn't then," said the junkman. "But I do now."

Jolly old Saint Orlo at the laughing stage after years of working himself to death to make Leini happy; the peace and wisdom of old age making him smile no matter how much his knees hurt, his back permanently wrenched after carting bathtubs from one end of the city to the other for his secret bride. In bad weather, his teeth hurt.

A year ago, in inexplicable sympathy with his adopted nation, Leini's husband had taken his life and Orlo hadn't stopped laughing since.

George was dead, dead, dead and Orlo—his mirth gurgling like a brook—didn't feel a whit of guilt.

"When?" asked Wigmann.

"Back in '55," said Orlo, chopping an onion. "Took the 2:12 Oriole Wing to New York City to see a Chinese witch doctor. He was going to cure what ailed us."

"I didn't say I was sick," said Wigmann.

Orlo remembered when he was Wigmann's age, the year Leini got married, a year into their affair. He'd sat brooding on the roof of the Salvage House as his lover's wedding guests danced in a circle behind Ralph's Lunch across the street.

He'd climbed his roof a week later to watch the lunch room burn to the ground, starting a heart-shaped hole into orange and gold flames as harbor winds fanned them toward downtown.

As youth fades, the world beats acceptance into you or kicks the life out of you.

"All I want to know is where the train is going and when it's gonna get there," said Wigmann.

"That's all?"

"I wish you'd stop laughing," said Wigmann, who couldn't remember his father laughing, even when something was funny.

When his mother wasn't laughing or crying, she was yelling or preaching or—until this year—asking her husband how he could sit for hours without changing the expression on his face.

"What makes you think I can answer these questions, Junior?"

"You're still making the pig's feet, aren't you?" said Wigmann, who'd always refused when his father tried to get him to taste one and always passed over the trotters that sweetened his mother's spaghetti sauce.

"Yes," chuckled Orlo. "That I am. You know what that goofy Chinaman wanted me to do when I asked these questions?"

"What?"

"Drink an antler crushed up inside a milkshake."

"And?"

"It was that or go home empty-handed."

(I'm not going home empty-handed, thought Wigmann. I'm getting married.)

"He said it would give us energy," said Orlo. "We wanted to have a baby."

"Barbara and I want children."

"Save your money on antlers," said Orlo. "It's cheaper just to love somebody."

"It didn't work?"

"There's a lot you could do with your time besides wait around for someone to see things your way," said Orlo. "Did you know the city wants to put an expressway through this neighborhood? They're already taking people's homes on Boston Street. Half the Polacks on the waterfront are dying of heartache. Those crooks offered me $6,000 for this place, take it or leave it. They want to come right across the harbor with a double-decker highway to block out the sun. A mile the other way and they'd be coming for your father's bar. We could use somebody like you to help us fight the sons-of-bitches."

Wigmann nudged the ruby to the side. Orlo turned down the flame under the figs on the stove and gathered up the salt and spices and onion to take outside.

"Did you hear what I said?"

Wigmann held up an emerald in a half-century old basket setting and said: "I'll take this one."

"For that much you could have the hair," said Orlo. "It'll be worth ten times as much long after that ring is gone."

"How much?"

"Emeralds crack easy," said Orlo. "Be careful with it."

"I will," said Wigmann, taking out his cash.

"Listen to me, Junior. Listen good. If they screw this part of town, Baltimore City is finished."

"I'm sorry Mr. Orlo," said Wigmann, slipping the ring in his pocket. "I can't concentrate right now."

More than all the stands of anticipation being braided in Little Basilio's imagination—his very pulse directed to the moment when guests would stream through the front door of his grandparents' house—was Wigmann's determination to avoid the evening.

Wigmann had been Basilio once. He'd walked through his Aunt Francesca's door with his parents and a warm dish and expectations, stuffing himself with treats while waiting for the clock to move.

But Wigmann wasn't a little boy anymore and he knew it as he left the Salvage House in a light snow, a car full of presents and an emerald ring in his pocket.

At the Broadway Market, Basilio helped his grandfather carry a hundred dollars worth of seafood: Scallops and oysters and snapper and the eel. Clams. A fat rockfish. Shrimp, squid, mussels, and smelts.

It was cold enough to let the fish sit in the car for a moment while Grandpop indulged Basilio in a visit to Kramer's, the candy store on Eastern Avenue where corn popped in the front window and an exhaust fan pushed the scent of hot caramel into the street; the smell of caramel and popped corn mixing with the clean, brisk wind blowing the snow.

The boy would do all of his shopping here and leave with a dozen paper bags of sweets across which he would letter names and draw pictures of birds and guitars and houses shaped like hearts.

Wigmann caught sight of the boy and his grandfather as he drove east along the Avenue and decided to give his mother the courtesy of a call, rattling change in his hand at a payphone across the street from Kramer's.

Above his head, the Great Bolewicki Depression Clock goaded him: "It's not too late to start your own tradition."

Sucking on a candy cane, Wigmann gave away three of the gifts left on his stoop to the first three people who walked by: a blind man drumming his fingernails against a metal pan rattling with change; a kid with a runny nose being dragged down the street by his mother; and a fat man in a Santa suit ringing a bell in front of Epstein's department store.

"Thanks," said the old buzzard. "Nobody thinks that Santa might like a present."

With one eye watching Basilio and his grandfather browse the candy store, Wigmann dropped a dime into the phone and called home.

"Hi Ma."

"What time did you leave this morning? I didn't even hear you go out. Lola said it was still dark out. I'm going to give her that artificial tree your father used to put up in the bar. You know that one? Silver and it changes colors when you shine a light on it."

"Any calls?"

"No."

"You sure?"

"What's the matter, hon? Ain't Barbara with you?"

Wigmann searched for his father's cool resolve.

"I need a favor, Junior."

"What Ma?"

"It's your Aunt Francie that needs the favor."

"What?"

"I don't know how my sister does it every year. All those people for a sit-down dinner. Please get there on time."

"Ma, what do you WANT?"

"Watch yourself."

"I'm sorry."

"Can you go down Pratt Street and pick up a Spanish guy off a ship?"

"It never ends."

"What's that?"

"Is the ship in yet?"

"I don't know. You have to check Pier Five. What's wrong, hon? I know you miss your father, we all do. But we've got to do the right thing and the next right thing is to help Aunt Francie."

"What's the name of the ship?"

"Hold on."

Wigmann's mother put down the phone and he could hear her rummaging upstairs from the saloon, picturing her in house coat and slippers. When she returned to the phone, Wigmann was munching on a bag of caramel popcorn.

"What are you eating?"

"Nothing."

"Junk? You're going to ruin your dinner."

"It is ruined."

"What?"

"The name of the ship, Ma. What's the name of the ship?"

"The *Galicia*. It's coming in from China."

"A slow boat?"

"What's that?"

"What pier, Mom?"

"Don't get funny with me mister. I don't know what pier."

"What's the man's name?"

"Mr. Steve. You remember Mr. Steve. He always brings gifts you can't get anywhere. Mr. Steve."

"I remember."

Wigmann hung up and leaned back to watch Basilio and his grandfather pull away from the candy store, wondering, in a swirl of flurries, if he should go down to Pratt Street or let Mr. Steve find his own way.

The two Basilios returned from their errands to find a letter from Spain wedged between the storm door and the front door of 627 South

Macon Street. Grandpop put the letter under his hat and carried in the food. Basilio ran upstairs to arrange his candy bags on the bureau beneath the skylight, drawing a name on each one.

Before he could smear the letters with milky glue and dust them with sparkles, he was called downstairs. On the way, he noticed the easel next to the Christmas tree in the front window.

Basilio's father and uncle had arrived while he was out, both in aprons. Oil bubbled in a deep fryer and knives were sharpened against whetstones, the better to scale the fish and slice their bellies. Dough for empanada had been rolled out. It was time to work.

Little Basilio was assigned the tricky task of helping and staying out of the way.

Don't get too close to the hot oil, they said, dropping anchovies wrapped in dough into the vat.

Stop picking at the dough.

Up and down the steps they marched him for the right spoon, a certain bowl, and the colander. A thousand times, up and down, a thousand passes by the idle easel.

Walk, they said, don't run.

Amuse yourself.

Be a good boy.

The preparations took most of the morning and all of the afternoon. Christmas linen folded and waiting. A pyramid of fruit sat in the center of the table as the snapper baked in the oven.

Basilio's father took off his apron, sent his son upstairs for a nap with a kiss on the head, and went home to clean up before returning with the rest of the family.

Like the screw of a great ship laboring against the current, Wigmann found himself on the parking lot of a green, ramshackle seafood house on Pratt Street to sit and wait and do what he was told.

He'd brought a few presents in from the car, the pile now reduced to a single package on the back seat as he walked through a stiff wind into Connolly's, taking an ice-cream parlor chair at a wobbly table covered with white cloth. Tortoise shells and seaman's knots hung on the pale green walls.

Wigmann set the gifts on the table and looked for a waitress. Aside from a few folks getting carry-out and a man shouldering a half-bushel of oysters to his car, the place was empty. A bus boy began setting chairs on top of the tables.

"I'll start with a beer," Wigmann said to the waitress, unwrapping one of the presents when she left and finding a paperback of *The Diary of a Young Girl*.

The oddity of the gift—a school kid's book about a Jewish girl to celebrate Christmas—made Wigmann wonder what else he'd given away.

Barbara had inscribed it: "Anne just wasn't some kid who kept a diary. She was a natural."

Flipping through the book as the waitress arrived with his beer, Wigmann found entries for late December and began reading.

"The Secret Annex has heard the joyful news that each person will receive an extra quarter of a pound of butter for Christmas. It says half a pound in the newspapers...but not for Jews who have gone into hiding."

"The oysters are good," said the waitress. "And the pan fried rock."

Wigmann scanned the menu, his headache fading with each sip of beer.

"Something heavy," said Wigmann. "Pork chops with mashed potatoes and gravy, a side order of baked beans, the cole slaw, and apple pie...oh yeah, and another beer."

The waitress left with the order and Wigmann paged forward to Anne's second Christmas in hiding as three red tugboats with white dots on their stacks pulled a freighter alongside a rotting pier across from the restaurant, *Galicia* stenciled across her bow.

"I couldn't help feeling a great longing to laugh until my tummy ached. Especially at this time of the year with all the holidays...when someone comes in from outside, with the wind in their clothes and the cold on their faces, then I could bury my head in the blankets to stop myself thinking: 'When will we be granted the privilege of smelling fresh air?'"

Outside, the air turned colder with the setting sun; a gray December cold that moved through the restaurant's concrete floor and into the soles of Wigmann's shoes as his food arrived.

Wigmann ate fast, searched for comforting passages in the diary, ordered another beer, and stuffed himself until he was nearly sick, aware that a blessing over the meal on Macon Street would be said before the hawser lines were made fast between the *Galicia* and Pier Five.

How many sins could you commit in one day and still tell yourself that you were a good man?

Wigmann paid the bill, scribbled the waitress's name across another present he'd brought to the table, shoved the diary in his back pocket, and ambled out into the glorious fresh air of Pratt Street to watch the *Galicia* tie up and wait for Mr. Steve to come down the gangway.

On the way, the pork chops heavy in his gut, Wigmann passed a payphone and dumped enough quarters into it to travel the distance he had not found the resolve to bridge in his car.

"Thank you for the presents," he said, jingling the ring in his pocket.

"I'm glad you liked them."

"I'm sorry," said Wigmann into the silent receiver.

He said: "Why don't I come up? I'll leave right now."

"No," said Barbara. "Don't."

In twos and threes they arrived. One at a time and in bunches.

Gloved hands knocking against a vestibule door sparkling with beveled glass as it opened and closed, open and closed; coats piled on a roll-away bed in the middle room, presents set beneath a small tree in the window of the parlor.

Basilio, scrubbed and dressed and waiting—the front room dark except for twinkling lights and shadows from the street—sat on the sofa and watched the parade come in the front door, troop to the kitchen at the back of the house, and head downstairs.

He sat accepting kisses and pinches and good wishes and dollar bills.

The boy enjoyed faces and committed the exaggerated features of the guests to memory—sagging ears and eyebrows like pompadours, the place where chins ended and necks began, breasts like feather pillows, and a sketch book's worth of noses.

Basilio sat with his hands folded in his lap, legs not long enough for his feet to touch the linoleum; the easel before him holding a blank sheet of newsprint.

His parents arrived with Jose Pepper, his little brother.

His cousin Donna showed up wearing a green velvet jumper and carrying a cardboard case with a plastic handle, the box filled with 45 rpm records; parents behind her, scooting her forward.

And then his grandmother's best friend—Miss Leini—came through the door with coloring books, Hershey bars wrapped in red foil, and a secret for her only girlfriend, a hand-picked treasure from her lover's Salvage House.

In the wink of an eye, 627 South Macon Street went from quiet and empty to noisy and full; the heat of the bodies intensifying the aroma of foods that had perfumed the house.

Aunt Lola and three of her sisters came in the back door from the alley.

"Merry Christmas!"

Once all of the grown-ups were downstairs, Basilio and Donna scoured the growing piles of presents for flat cardboard squares that could only be one thing—long-playing record albums—but did not find any.

No rock and roll until after dinner. That was the rule. But because it was Christmas and everyone was happy, the kids could act up a little bit.

"Children!" came the call from the basement. "Come down and take your seats."

Grandpop covered his face with his hands to pray over the meal and one of the Bombacci sisters took a frond of palm, dipped it in a mayonnaise jar of holy water she carried in her purse, and walked around the table sprinkling a blessing on more than two dozen people, the kids getting two or three shakes for good measure.

Basilio dabbed at the water that landed behind his ear to taste it.

It tasted like water.

From the front of the basement to the back, tables were crowded with bowls of food, platters of food, trays of food, plates of food. Homemade pasta with red sauce and tuna; homemade pasta with white sauce and clams; celery sticks dipped in shallow dishes of olive oil and black pepper; roasted chestnuts; a codfish stew with potatoes and peas; the empanada with "1964" baked into the crust; rockfish stuffed with crab and bread crumbs; salty "lupini" beans you popped out of their transparent yellow husks; red snapper topped with slices of lemon and onion; steamed shrimp; stuffed clams; the fantastic eel; artichoke hearts baked with bread crumbs and butter.

The desserts covered a side table. Italian nougat—vanilla, orange, and lemon—called torrone; stacks of pungent pizzelles; raisin squares; custard rimmed with caramel; crusty bread made soft with red wine and sweet with sugar.

After taking his hands from his face, plates and bowls circling the table, everyone helping to their fill, Grandpop pulled the letter from

Spain out of his pocket and read it to the crowd in English.

Rings of fluorescent light on the ceiling caught the Spaniard's smile as he came to an announcement.

"We have in our family new life," he said. "A girl named Nieves."

Everyone raised a glass to toast the news, the children given juice glasses filled half with wine and half with Lemo-Nizer soda pop.

"Salud!"

The envelope from Spain circled the table and when it came to Basilio his eyes glazed at the colors on the stamps—red and gold—and he ran his fingers over the Old World script.

"He'll be here," Wigmann's mother kept saying. "Don't you worry."

Wigmann stood at the foot of the gangway making small talk with the man on watch while waiting for Mr. Steve. The watchman looked up at the dark sky as he talked, at peace with a seaman's knowledge that he would see Christmas arrive from a folding chair on a pier an ocean from his home.

"Yep," said Wigmann. "I'm going to drop the old swabbie off, drive straight through the night, and ask her to marry me."

"Good luck," said the watchman.

Wigmann took Anne's diary from his back pocket—the moon and a cross of white lights on the ship's stack glowing in the dark circles under the author's eyes—and handed it to the watchman when Mr. Steve appeared at the top of the gangway with a duffel bag on his shoulder.

Wigmann drove east on Lombard Street, past smokehounds passing a jug around a fire in a barrel at the Fallsway; east toward the orange brick rowhouses of Highlandtown where Basilio was being told he must taste a bit of every dish on the table.

"How many children?" Mr. Steve asked.

"Where?"

"Tonight. How many children waiting?"

"At least three," said Wigmann. "But there could be a house full of them."

"Good," laughed Mr. Steve, his pockets jingling with silver coins. "Fill the house."

By the time Wigmann passed the Baker Whitely tugboats on Thames Street and made it around the harbor to the canning factories in Canton, the dishes from the first course had been cleared and the three waiting children—Basilio, Donna, and Jose Pepper—had been excused from the table.

Upstairs, they were joined at the record player by a neighborhood girl named Trudy whose parents had just divorced.

Jose Pepper sat next to the portable stereo, more interested in how it worked than the music coming out of it; Basilio and Donna took turns putting on their favorite songs, the curtains drawn in the front window, the tiny tree shining out to the street as Wigmann pulled to the curb, deciding that he had to help Mr. Steve in with his bag and say hello to his mother.

Kneeling outside the basement window to glimpse the celebration on the other side of the glass, Wigmann watched the meal begin anew with each fresh face that came down the steps.

He imagined himself seated between his old man and Barbara at the table, explaining the different foods to her as the plates passed by.

Wigmann's seat was empty, his plate unsoiled and his father's spot occupied by a heavy-set man from the Canary Islands peeling chestnuts with a penknife. His mother sat close to her sisters and turned toward the steps every other moment to see if it was her son's footsteps she heard.

Wigmann belched, stood up with Mr. Steve's bag under one arm and the last present from Barbara in the other, and went inside. The house was warm with familiar smells, memories overwhelming a big baby who'd spent all day stuffing himself with distractions.

"Here," said Wigmann, handing the last package—obviously a

record—to Donna, who ripped the paper and cried: "The Beatles!"

(Why them? Wigmann wondered. The Fab Four owned the world, Mr. Orlo was proof of that, but their joy hadn't played a part in his and Barbara's courtship anymore than Anne's suffering.)

"Put it on!" said Basilio, hoping Santa would be as good to him.

Donna spun the record—"Beatles '65"—and Wigmann took her by the hand for a dance, gliding the girl around the room on the top of his shoes.

Trudy jumped up and down with Jose Pepper, and Basilio, sketching out the scene at his easel, didn't understand that what he was feeling was jealousy.

Downstairs, Mr. Steve took a string of dried figs from his pocket and spread them out. A five-year-old chased a three-year-old around the table. Glasses were refilled, dishes washed and dried and used again.

Catching the Mersey beat as it pulsed through the floorboards—"I'm so glad that she's my little girl..."—Mr. Steve lit a long cigar and called for the children and his bag. The kids raced down the steps—strange guests were always giving children something on Macon Street—and Wigmann lumbered after them with the seaman's bag.

"There you are!" cried Wigmann's mother. "Sit down. Eat."

Wigmann grabbed a beer out of the refrigerator, kissed his mother on the cheek, and stood with the children near Mr. Steve.

After giving the youngest kids at the table silver coins, the Spaniard dug deep in his bag and brought out a box of cigars, a bottle of Fundador cognac, a handful of unwrapped baubles, and then, one after another, to squeals of delight, dolls of four young men with mop-top haircuts.

Made in Japan, no store or kid in America had such treasures.

"One for you," said Mr. Steve, handing the Paul doll to Donna. "And you," he said, giving Ringo to Jose Pepper, "and for you," as Trudy embraced George.

"And," he said, extending John Lennon to Basilio, "for you."

"Dolls for a boy," scoffed Grandpop.

"They're kids," said his wife.

"You should eat a little something and take the kids over to see the trains," said Wigmann's mother.

Taking the doll from his son, Basilio's father ran his hands over John's head and declared it a toy for sissies as the boy grabbed the doll back.

Lifelike down to the dimples, there was something odd about the dolls. Instead of arms holding guitars, the toys had wings—thin, holographic webbing of translucent plastic shaped like maple seedlings.

"They fly," said Mr. Steve, showing how they worked.

"They fly!" cried Jose Pepper, jumping up and down.

"Like angels," said Mr. Steve.

Inside the doll boxes were launching pistols with zip cords. The feet fit into the pistols and when you pulled the cord, the doll twirled into the air. The harder you pulled, the higher they flew.

"A flying Beatle," marveled a guest as Ringo helicoptered from one end of the table to the other.

In a moment, nearly all of the adults were taking turns with the dolls.

Watching the Beatles fly around the basement, Leini imagined the sex she'd enjoy when the other women walked to Midnight Mass with their children and grandchildren.

Picking up fried tentacles of squid—saving her appetite for a secret delicacy, trying not to worry about what she and the junkman would do if the city knocked the Salvage House down—she felt no guilt.

Not a whit of regret about her husband's suicide as she reached out to catch George as he sailed by.

While the others clamored to take the next turn—the kids jumping up and down, pulling at the hem of Leini's black dress—the widow stared into the sweet face of the quiet Beatle and savored a wistful peace.

"Do you want to know a secret?" she hummed. "Do you promise not to tell?"

Leini handed the doll to Basilio and asked Mr. Steve where she could get a set.

"Hell," said Basilio's other grandmother, a Polish seamstress. "By Easter they'll have shelves of 'em up Epstein's."

Mr. Steve leaned toward Leini with the self-assured smile that the Greek—still a beauty at fifty-five—only saw in the faces of Europeans. He said there were not any more to be had and offered her a peeled chestnut.

"Not only did somebody figure out how to make them fly, but made sure they flew beautifully," said Trudy's father, a mechanic at Crown Cork & Seal. "That's about as close to intangible as you can get."

Beautifully they flew until a sugar bowl fell to the floor, a glass of wine tipped over, a baby who wanted a turn started to squeal, and Grandpop slapped his palm against the table.

"What are we?" he demanded. "Americans?"

"Okay kids," said Basilio's mother, getting up to percolate a pot of coffee. "Take them upstairs."

Wigmann grabbed another beer from the refrigerator, told his mother for the third time that he wasn't hungry, and followed the children up the steps.

The kids ran out into the cold with the dolls and Wigmann trooped out after them with his beer.

For all of their enthusiasm, Trudy and Donna and Jose Pepper were tentative pulling their strings; Paul, George, and Ringo barely rising higher than the wire fence before falling near their feet.

It was Basilio's turn and for some reason—a vague feeling akin to the one he felt watching Donna dance with Wigmann, something close to the shame that burned when his father called the Beatles sissies—Basilio yanked the cord with all of his might and John shot into space as if fired from a gun.

Their heads tilted back, the children watched as the doll cleared the trees, and then the rooftops, soared beyond the chimneys and into the clouds and then—as though the stars reached down to receive him—John Lennon was assumed into the heavens over Highlandtown.

"Wow!" said Donna.

"Geezy," said Jose Pepper.

Wigmann whistled and Basilio began to cry.

"It's okay," said Wigmann, grateful for the most beautiful thing he'd seen all day. "We'll find it."

"I'm cold," said Trudy, picking up her doll and going inside.

"Me too," said Jose Pepper.

"Basilio," said Donna, rushing in the house and running back out. "Take your coat."

Basilio wiped his nose, put on his coat, and followed Wigmann into the alley.

"Don't worry," said Wigmann. "I knew a girl who had as much talent as you but her family was in such a bad way at Christmas that Santa brought just enough butter to make a few biscuits."

"I don't want biscuits," said Basilio.

(We are Americans, thought Wigmann.)

"I know you don't," he said, scouring the backyards and trees for the doll. "I'm just telling you how it is sometimes."

At the end of the alley, Wigmann got an idea and sat Basilio down on a set of cold marble steps across the street from the beer garden.

"Stay here," he said before slipping into the saloon, running to the top floor, and opening a small hatch in the ceiling that led to the roof.

His teeth chattering, Basilio watched Wigmann's silhouette zig-zag across the rooftops as he checked rain gutters and chimneys, searching from one end of the block to the other in vain before appearing before the shivering boy with regrets.

Taking Basilio by the hand, Wigmann walked into the bar, hit the lights, poured the kid a Coke, and punched up "She Loves You" on the jukebox before dumping the bowl of soggy ginger snaps in the trash.

Wigmann pulled down an eight-foot-by-eight-foot wooden garden from the wall—five trains circling three platforms, farm houses, a town square with a water fountain and miniature Ferris wheel—and turned the bar into a carnival.

"Maybe the Beatles are just for girls," said Basilio.

"Something tells me the grown-ups are wrong on this one," said Wigmann. "Just like some people will tell you that nobody eats sauerkraut at Christmas, but I do."

"You're a grown-up," said Basilio.

"Only because I'm older than you," said Wigmann.

Leaving the boy alone with the trains, Wigmann walked behind the bar and ducked into his bedroom. A moment later, he approached Basilio with open palms; a lock of brown hair in one hand and a swatch of bedsheet in the other.

"Merry Christmas!"

"What is it?"

"Stuff that's going to be worth a million dollars because of a million kids like you."

"Hair?"

"John's."

Basilio's heart jumped.

"No."

"Yes."

"Where'd you get it?"

"When they were here." said Wigmann. "I know somebody."

Wondering how you could know anyone that important, Basilio pointed to Wigmann's other hand.

"It's a piece of the sheets they slept on at the Holiday Inn, the one with the revolving restaurant on top," Wigmann said. "Room 1013."

Wigmann told Basilio to put his hands out and set the lock of hair and the linen in the boy's palms as the bells of Holy Redeemer began ringing for Midnight Mass.

Folding the boy's fingers around the goodies, he said: "They're yours."

"All mine?"

"To keep."

"Can I tell anybody?"

"They might not believe you," said Wigmann. "Hey, listen...I think they're calling for you."

Walking Basilio out to the alley, Wigmann handed the boy over to a parade of women and children making their way to church.

"Just showing him the trains," he said as Basilio skipped into line with Donna and Jose Pepper, hands tight around the frankincense and myrrh in his pocket.

"You coming?" asked Wigmann's mother.

"Nah. You say a few prayers for me," he said, giving her a hug.

Back inside, Wigmann grabbed a beer from the cool box and watched the trains run, twinkling lights glinting off a cracked emerald ring and a pair of scissors laying open on his bed.

There was once a room of velvet here . . .

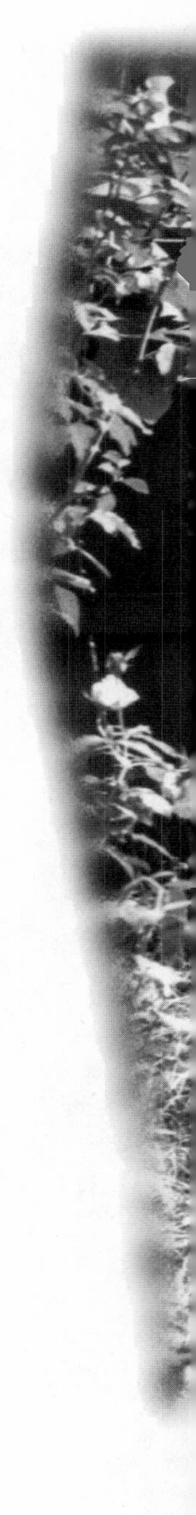

The Legend of the Velvet Room

Trixie Loo arrived in Patterson Park at dawn as a hundred hotair balloons rose like new tulips for a Memorial Day race across the clear blue skies of the Holy Land.

She had a reporter's notebook in her back pocket and carried a cup of coffee, the youngest in a West Coast family of scientists humoring their Ivy League baby through a season of slumming.

Trixie was new in Baltimore—ambition bristling, hair shorn less than a quarter-inch from her scalp—and the balloon race was her first assignment in a hard-won summer internship at *The Sun*, the paper of Mencken and Schoettler and Maulsby.

She was up against a phalanx of other kids competing for the one, full-time staff job awarded at the end of each summer and she had the competition sized up.

Stepping through the crowd, she had an eye out for her photographer and—in the midst of corporate-sponsored balloons that looked like beer bottles and computers and cell phones—a bag of hot air shaped like the head of Elvis Presley.

You didn't need a journalism degree to know that the King made good copy.

Coming upon Elvis as the balloon reached its full height, Trixie found a teenage girl sitting in the wicker gondola.

"What's your name?"

"Ruth."

"Ruth what?"

"Ruth."

"Are you excited?"

"Of course," the girl replied as the pilot loosened the tethers holding the eighty-foot marvel to the Earth. "But how are you going to tell people how exciting it is standing around watching?"

Trixie stood nailed to the ground.

"Let me go with you," she said.

"Too late," said the pilot, throwing off the last weight.

"Too late," laughed Ruthie.

Head tilted back, her eyes shielded from the sun, Trixie watched Elvis rise through the clouds, sharp light behind the princess in the gondola, illuminating her nut-brown hair and a perfectly shaped head; more beauty than any newspaper could hold.

"Psst, Missie," asked a little man dressed like a clown, a gnarled ganef in a goof's suit pulling at Trixie's shirt. "You want to bag a real story before it's gone for good?"

Ted the Clown led Trixie a half-mile south from Patterson Park to a narrow waterfront lane where a derelict slaughterhouse faced a row of broken rowhouses.

Three bulldozers and a crane crowded the alley, the air thick with the dust of bricks laid more than a hundred-and-fifty years ago.

All across the city, blocks of boarded-up and abandoned houses—dens of fiends and prostitutes and thieves—were crumbling like stale crackers.

The former homes of working people who'd died or moved away were now sanctuary for the Monster that Ate Baltimore City.

On Cabbage Alley, a crowd watched walls wobble like taffy, mortar returning to sand as one house after another pitched into the street.

Trixie pushed through the crowd for a better look, reaching the curb as a wrecking ball smacked the side of the slaughterhouse, sending the concrete head of an ornamental pig to her feet.

"All they know how to do these days is tear things down," said an old Czech with a kerchief on her head. "Christ, the whole city's falling apart."

"This used to be a nice place to live," said a great-grandmother who'd grown up shucking oysters in the alley.

"Yeah," laughed a man next to her. "When Coolidge was president."

Trixie picked the pig's head out of the gutter and asked the clown where the story was.

"A paradise was here," said Ted. "A velvet Eden."

"Schaefer wouldn't let this happen if he was mayor," said a black man.

"Schaefer ain't mayor."

"Why don't they just flatten the whole city and bring the Amish down to grow corn?"

"Give the whole kit-and-caboodle back to the Indians."

"It's a shame."

"A goddamn shame."

A shrew in her nineties leaned on her cane and pointed a crooked finger toward the middle of the block.

"See that skinny yellow house. The one they ain't torn all the way down yet? My grandmother used to tell me stories about the ragman and the little Greek girl he kept prisoner there. The only thing he'd give her to eat was pig guts from the butcher shop."

"Shut up!"

The scream pierced the rumble of the bulldozers, a shrill keening from a strange bird at the back of the crowd; a woman with bad eyes, something wrong with the sockets and the brow.

"Shut up and leave 'em in peace for Christ's sake."

Trixie scribbled in her notebook: Eyes too close together or too far apart? Yellow house. City dying. People disturbed.

The clown whispered: "A paradise..."

"Where?"

Ted pointed to the house where the ragman kept his quarry.

"Prove it," said Trixie.

"Everybody knows."

The bulldozers stopped, leaving the yellow house and the one next to it standing as the men knocked off for the day.

Trixie searched for the cock-eyed woman in vain.

"Who was that?"

"Your story," said the clown.

Trixie swept into the newsroom, sat the cracked pig's head on the City Desk, grabbed a diet soda, and sat down to write.

It was only a balloon race, but it was Trixie's first byline at *The Sun* and she intended to knock it over the fence.

"Welcome aboard," said the weekend editor. "We've got great art of the balloons. They're taking a picture out front."

"What about the story?"

"Inside local."

Shit, thought Trixie, staring at a blank computer screen, writing the story as if it were going A1/ anyway, cramming it with detail and description; the way the tarred rooftops of East Baltimore looked on a warm day in late May as a rainbow of nylon bulbs rose above them.

She began with a snapshot of the morning sun shining through the folds of Ruthie's ears as the billowing head of Elvis Presley floated up to heaven, the veins in the teenager's ears an intricate network of violet, just a shade lighter than Trixie's prose.

Flipping through her notes, Trixie came across "Little Leini" scrawled across a page, followed by scraps for which she'd traded the clown a shot of brandy at a saloon around the corner from Cabbage Alley.

"Daughter...velvet...junk shop/Clinton Street...weird eyes...pig's feet..."

Trixie finished the balloon story as the night editor arrived.

"All yours, Alvarez," said the weekend editor. "Everything has moved except a couple of obits. There's a brief on a nickel-and-dime murder coming and the intern's got a balloon feature for the first edition."

"Got it," said Alvarez, sipping coffee.

"Oh yeah, and don't forget to set the lottery numbers. You forgot last night."

"Right."

Alvarez stood up and called across the room.

"You Loo?"

The girl nodded and he summoned her to the chair next to his desk.

"Rafael Alvarez," he said.

Trixie shook his hand, sat down, and inhaled a strong, sour odor beneath a veneer of aftershave and toothpaste.

"This is very good," said Alvarez, his palms sweating.

"Thank you."

"But it could be better."

Sick, haunted, and old at forty-two, Alvarez was considerate with the girl's copy; tightening it up, smoothing it out, patiently explaining what he was doing and why. Across the newsroom, the editor of the paper—a contemporary of Alvarez's named Arbitrari—read a copy of Loo's story and moved her star up a notch.

It was exceptional work for a kid Loo's age, Princess Ruthie worthy of a series herself. While Alvarez left most of Trixie's prose intact, he urged her to play it straighter next time.

Good writing is built upon precision and restraint, he told the plain-faced girl, impressed with her spunk, struggling not to stare at her scalp and praying for the chance to get a quick belt between editions down at the House of Welsh.

Alvarez watched something honest move across Trixie's face as she mouthed phrases from the story she especially liked. It reminded him of his lost self. He said: "The distance between the right word and the almost right word...," and lost his train of thought.

"Yes?" said Trixie.

"What?"

"The difference between the right word and the almost right word?"

"Oh yeah. It's the difference between lightning and the lightning bug."

Jesus, thought Alvarez, it happened again.

"Did you make that up?"

"No. I'm asking if you can hear the music in the commas."

"The commas?"

"Yeah."

"Who is this lunatic?" thought Trixie.

She said: "I found a good story when I was out today."

"What?"

"They're tearing down the city."

"No shit."

Trixie was silent.

"Poof!" said Alvarez. "Fresh prairies for a vanishing populace."

"It's not funny."

"Who said it was?"

"I want to write about it."

"We write about it every day, three paragraphs at a time: No witnesses, no motive, no suspects."

"Somebody told me that people who used to live in the houses they're tearing down are dying of heartbreak," said Trixie. "I want to write it from their point of view."

"Go for it."

"Really?"

"Absolutely."

Alvarez's computer beeped and he told Trixie that Arbitrari wanted to see her, prompting a look from Loo as if she'd been summoned to the principal's office. He thought he saw her tremble, but it could have been his vision.

"Tell him your idea," he said. "It's a good one."

Alvarez watched Trixie walk across the newsroom and wished he still cared enough to go out in the streets of his hometown and document what was happening to it.

"Sweet kid," he thought. "Stupid haircut."

Arbitrari welcomed Trixie into his office with praise.

"This could be a big summer for you," he said.

"I hope so."

"Nail everything that moves," said Arbitrari. "And work on your writing."

"I have an idea," said Trixie.

Arbitrari put his feet on his desk. "Let's hear it."

"It looks to me like they're trying to bulldoze Baltimore into an open field," said Trixie. "And nobody seems to know what to do next."

Arbitrari nodded.

"Even in California, people know that rowhouses are Baltimore's identity and when a city loses its identity, it's dead," said Trixie. "This morning we ran this quote from one of the demolition contractors: 'We've made more money blowing things up in Baltimore this year than we have in the whole country in the last five years.'"

"Go for it," said Arbitrari.

"You mean it?"

"Keep your editors happy and keep me posted. When you think you've got enough to start writing we'll talk. How are people treating you?"

"Mr. Alvarez is interesting."

Arbitrari walked to his office window and looked across the newsroom at the night editor as Alvarez cracked the seal on a miniature of vodka under his desk and tipped it into a cup of black coffee.

"I came up with him," said Arbitrari. "Ralphie had more talent than any five people we've got now."

"What happened?"

"I'll tell you sometime," said Arbitrari. "Keep up the good work."

As she left the newsroom, Trixie glanced at Alvarez and flipped through her notes to the page with "Cabbage Alley" scrawled across the top.

Were the angry woman's eyes too close together?

Or too far apart?

Trixie woke early the next morning, a Sunday, and drove to Cabbage Alley to sift the rubble for clues, puzzling an analogy offered by a flack at City Hall.

As a blue crab matures, it sheds its obsolete shell and moves on.

The city, he told Trixie, is moving on.

Conservative estimates put the number of abandoned rowhouses in Baltimore at forty thousand. Some twelve hundred people left every month.

"We tried to re-settle Bosnian refugees here but they only stayed a month or so before moving to the county," the flack had said. "Even victims of ethnic cleansing don't want to live in Baltimore City."

Church bells pealed as Trixie parked on Eastern Avenue, the streets as empty as the beer bottles balanced on the curbs. Dirt blew off the wreckage of Cabbage Alley.

Most of 408 Cabbage Alley remained, the missing front wall revealing a crooked set of stairs to the second floor. Holding onto a splintered banister, Trixie ascended the ruins, stepping carefully, whispering: "There was once a room of velvet here..."

A room that disappeared from the world before she was born.

Wind blew through the building, rustling the bristles on Trixie's scalp as she reached the top to survey a nearly empty room. Morning sun shone through holes in the ceiling, holes in the floor, holes in the walls; sparkling across dirt and dead bugs and a stucco of syringes and pigeon shit.

Addicts had ripped everything out except a filthy claw-foot tub against a wall, its bulk too great for the most desperate junkie.

Trixie pushed through French doors, every pane broken, and thought of filling the empty squares with Chinese glass. She stepped onto a balcony stripped of its iron railing, the backyard thick with brambles, wild roses, ivy, weeds, and stout-trunked fig trees spreading across the width of the yard.

Eden gone amok a half-mile from downtown.

Against a soaring brick wall at the back of the yard, Trixie saw remnants of mortar in the shape of copulating triangles, geometry that looked as though it had been scratched into the wall by visitors from another planet.

What, thought Trixie, going through her J-school catechism.

Who? When? Where?

Editing her copy, Alvarez had asked: "Can you frame the question?"

Trixie backed away from the edge and walked into the house remembering the fig preserves her great-grandmother made and promised to come back when the fruit was ripe. She thought of Nigh-Nigh's velvet sofa back in San Francisco; deep, rich burgundy with orange piping, the couch where Trixie took naps as a little girl, still there on Duncombe Street with the fig jam, worn and threadbare in a tiny apartment cluttered with Chinese newspapers and flowers growing out of jelly jars.

A velvet sofa, yes.

But an entire room?

Maybe in a Wild West whorehouse or the waiting rooms of the Chinatown herb doctors who worked magic along the alleys where the Loos had landed a hundred years before, where they'd gathered every Sunday when Trixie was little, when she'd hurry through dinner to sit on Nigh-Nigh's velvet sofa, reading quietly and running her fingertips across the cushions.

Trixie found a butterknife on the floor and began working the doors off their hinges, wondering where she'd hang them at the end of the summer when she snared the full-time reporter's job and got a decent apartment.

How good they'll look, she thought, leading to a study filled with books and a velvet love seat.

(Trixie was good with tools. She had the good hands and steady eye of her father, the surgeon who'd been telling his daughter since she was a little girl that she could be anything she wanted.)

Trixie began edging down the steps with the doors, easing them along the twisting, rickety stairs through a narrow, open well when an emaciated man covered with sores rushed her with a sledgehammer, a wild-eyed fuck with open cuts on his face and pus running from holes in his arms.

He'd come for the tub.

"Aaaah!" screamed Trixie, falling backward; tailbone banging the steps, her body tangled in the addict's filth as her shaved head smacked one riser after the other; shards of glass ripping her arms, blood from the man's loose scabs mixing with her own as they fell with the doors, the sledgehammer striking Trixie on the shins and knees, her notebook falling behind a hole in the plaster and the addict stomping on her ankle as he fled.

Lifting herself up, Trixie sucked in her tears, hobbled to her car, and drove away.

Trixie spent the rest of the day in the emergency room of Mercy Hospital while Alvarez, with a quart-and-a-half of vodka in him, sat at his kitchen table crooning Brian Wilson lyrics to his dusty cabinets.

"I wish you'd listen when I tell you now, baby let your hair grow long...it hurts inside to see you suffer now baby let your hair grow long there's something missing baby let your hair grow long..."

Alvarez's head dropped to the table and he rolled it from side-to-side against the Formica, trying to conjure a room of velvet in a whirlpool of vagaries.

"I'll help her," he mumbled through spittle.

Lifting his head, he roared: "I'll save her!" and fell backward, screaming at the cobwebs as he hit the floor.

"I'll save poetry and art and bald-headed little girls and motherfuck the news!!!"

Choking back bile and sour saliva, Alvarez wet himself and laughed—"I'll save the world..."—before passing out.

Trixie had chosen journalism in grade school, a declaration, at eight, of something that belonged to her and not the family.

The Sun was her first chance to prove to Mommy and Daddy that she could measure up; her shot, after four especially expensive years of college, to succeed with language the way her mother had done with a microscope and her father with a scalpel.

But with each bump of her head against the splintered wooden steps on Cabbage Alley, Trixie's waltz with the Monster that Ate Baltimore City diluted her hard-nosed investigation of a vanishing city into a brackish dream.

Leaving Mercy Hospital, she trembled with fear that the addict had infected her and burned to prove what no one thought important.

Arrogance melting into awkwardness.

From Woodward to Wordsworth.

Prosecutor to poet.

Trixie took Monday off to soak her ankle, re-wrap the bandage on her knee, change the dressings on her stitches, bathe her wounds, and ponder the best way to tell the story of a city's death.

The next day, she swung into the newsroom on crutches and

found herself on desk duty until she could get around again; half of the staff on vacation and Trixie used as utility: rewrite and cops and obits; working weather stories by phone, taking messages, and manning the night desk with Alvarez.

When there weren't any obits to write or cop calls to make, she translated press releases into briefs filed three paragraphs at a time, the other interns viewing Trixie's misfortune as one less byline to crowd theirs out of the paper.

Thrown together in a pack from universities across the country, the ambitious youngsters coupled, gossiped, believed they were better than they were, uncoupled, and recoupled while clawing their way past each other.

Virtually incapable of putting together a half-foot of seaworthy paragraphs, they bowed before Arbitrari and stabbed each other in the back for shots at A1.

Along the way, they discovered the Good Love, a bar on the gentrified side of the waterfront, walking distance from Cabbage Alley. The interns made it their special place. Trixie kept to herself and spent all of her time trading e-mail with Rafael Alvarez and tracking down anyone who lived within three blocks of Cabbage Alley.

"Did you know the family that lived around the corner?"

"Hon, there ain't been a family down there for thirty years."

"Is there anyone around who used to?"

"How the hell should I know?"

She asked on crutches, from the window of her car, at the grocery, and at the bank; she sat on white marble steps in the evening to make small talk and began having her clothes dry cleaned and her oil changed in the orbit of Eastern Avenue and Broadway to increase her chance of bumping into someone who remembered.

"Sorry, hon," they said. "We already get the paper."

The other interns cultivated sources among civil servants, city laborers, community do-gooders, First Amendment freaks, and neighborhood busy-bodies.

The only informant Trixie was able to cultivate wore white face and hit people up for change.

"This the Sunpapers? I need Trixie. Trixie Loo. You have her call Ted. She'll know. The clown. Ted the Clown. I got a tip for her. You tell her to call."

Alvarez loved Trixie's stories about the rum-pot clown and the woman with eyes like a flounder and the phantom velvet lovers and he encouraged her to run with them.

As Loo regaled him with her adventures through slaughterhouses and pigeon coops, Alvarez guided her to fiction he wished he'd written—"The Fountain of Highlandtown"—and journalism—"The Hoodle Patrol"—that aspired to fiction.

He cut her loose on slow nights and tried to keep her name in the paper.

"You check on the cop on life support at Hopkins?"

"Still critical."

"Anything for the final?"

"Just the kid who drowned trying to ride his bike down the Jones Falls."

"State Police?"

"Quiet. Want to get a drink after work?"

"Can't."

Trixie was not beautiful, not by a stretch, but she was young and vibrant and Alvarez thought more than once what it would be like to stand behind her and run his palm across the stubble on her head.

"Coffee?"

"Sorry."

Alvarez refused all of Trixie's requests except when she asked for advice on her project: more than eight thousand rowhouses bulldozed in Baltimore in three short years; thousands more awaiting the wrecking ball; nearly one-hundred thousand abandoned in all, the only thing standing between City Hall and a desert on the Patapsco.

"I want to build the story around the junkman and his lover."

"Why?"

"To show people what they're losing."

"Don't you think," said Alvarez, "that they already know?"

Trixie hadn't written a poem since the sixth grade, when she'd been named class wit at the most exclusive prep school in San Francisco.

But now, brooding on the City Desk with a busted leg, the exercise was a salve scribbled in a reporter's notebook.

"A swirling skirt of stars in a long, narrow room; bed beneath skylight at noon...smiles and skin of sun...her wage of sin...not pig's feet every time..."

The phone rang six times before Trixie snapped out of it.

"City Desk."

"How's Tricks?"

"What do *you* want, Ted?"

"No, cookie buns. What do you want?"

"Get to the point."

"Got a number for you. Old lady who lived across the street from the room. That's right. *The* room. Minnie's bedroom looked right into it."

"Minnie?"

"Minnie Fischer. Rode clear-cross the yoo-nited States in a motor-sickle during Prohibition."

"Where is she?"

"Sick, Tricks. She's real sick."

"Where, Ted?"

"Weak. On the edge."

"What do you want?"

"The usual."

"Give me her number, you worm."

"Now, now."

"The number Ted."

The clown spit it out and Trixie promised to drop off a bottle on her way home.

Hanging up, she opened the city crisscross directory and there, next to the telephone number Ted had given her, was Mildred Fischer at 409 Cabbage Alley where no one ever answered the door.

"She'll die young...and yearn beneath the neighborhood's pressing eyes...this kettlecloth world of stain will lift her stars like wind for a junkman's hand to heal...sometimes they stood on the balcony and shared an orange, ribbons of rind falling to the ground..."

As Trixie circled the City Desk, trying to put weight on her bad leg, two reporters rushed out of the newsroom to attend a hastily called press conference on a Department of Public Works strike that had halted everything in the city, including the decimation of Cabbage Alley.

"Loo, you up for an obit?"

Shit, thought Trixie, stuffing the poem in her pocket with Minnie Fischer's address and rubbing her aching knee.

A clerk handed Trixie a slip of paper with the number for the Chonjacki Funeral Home, the word "deceased," and next to it: "Minnie Fischer, old Baltimore."

The obit ran on B6 without a byline.

Limping her way through East Baltimore with a blank notebook full of anger over the death of Minnie Fischer, Trixie scoured the waterfront for surviving cannery workers, longshoreman, and oyster shuckers; aggravating her knee in pursuit of bean snippers.

"Try Binney Street," the clown said as Trixie bought him a beer. He quaffed another and threw back a shot. "Orlo was well-known on Grundy Street. And don't forget north of the park. Orlo did a hell of a business on Monument Street back when Charlie Logue had his bike shop there..."

Trixie knocked hard enough to rattle doors in their hinges, followed the weakest of leads and listened to old people who had nothing to do with Orlo and Leini talk about their aches and pains until she wanted to choke them.

After long days of sweating onto her notes and smearing the ink, she'd haul her skinny ass into the newsroom for the night shift and tell Alvarez every little thing.

"I don't have enough to write yet."

"That's all right," he'd say. "Keep going."

In her third week on the job, Trixie accepted Ted the Clown's offer of introduction to the woman with the unsettling eyes. A fist around his payment, Ted led Trixie down to the end of Clinton Street and onto the front porch of the Salvage House. He chanted a few scraps of ritual and disappeared.

Trixie opened the screen door onto a large parlor crowded with the discarded contents of Baltimore's attics, garages, and basements; entire walls made from stacks of books; cigar store Indians and Pirate Petes in every corner, live birds on their shoulders. An entire wall of manual typewriters. She walked gingerly to a counter where the woman who'd wailed as the wrecking ball laid low Cabbage Alley sat sorting religious medals into the compartments of a tackle box.

From the ceiling above her head hung a pair of stainless steel letters—an enormous "O" and an "L" just as big—taken from the facade of a demolished ballpark on 33rd Street consecrated as a memorial to a forgetful nation's war dead.

"Excuse me," said Trixie.

The woman looked up to meet Trixie's gaze.

"I'm a reporter for *The Sun*. I saw you the other day on Cabbage Alley."

"I know who you are."

"And, and..."

"And?"

"And I was wondering if you knew anything about a room on that block made out of velvet."

"No."

"Somebody said..."

"They lied."

"So," said Trixie, pointing to the stainless steel letters, unable to bring forth the names they stood for.

"So nothing," said Little Leini, returning to her work.

One day in late June, Trixie showed up for work and was dispatched to the courthouse for the trial of the Monster that Ate Baltimore City—an animal named Feather who'd lured a fifteen-year-old girl to the 29th Street Bridge with promises of good marijuana before devouring her.

A verdict was expected in less than an hour and while the jury thought it over, Trixie went to the land records office to search titles to properties in the 400 block of Cabbage Alley.

While combing through deeds written in longhand with a fountain pen, Trixie missed the jury foreman hand the bailiff a note that said "guilty"; missed the Monster smile at his victim's family as he shuffled away in chains; and missed the judge set a date for sentencing. Missed it all for an index card that led to Eastern Avenue, just off of Broadway.

Elbaum Brothers Properties was a rowhouse real estate office with a shyster's shingle, scarred wooden furniture, and rotted orange linoleum peeling away from the floor.

It looked like a pool hall in a 1930s' gangster movie.

Trixie peered through the glass and saw men shooting billiards, playing cards, and reading newspapers. Opening the heavy door, she walked inside to whoops and hollers greeting the results of the seventh race at Pimlico.

Hopeless, by a hair.

"May I help you?" said a man behind the counter, assuming that Trixie was a college student looking for a cheap apartment near the bars in Fells Point.

Trixie identified herself as a reporter and everyone looked up.

"You are?" said a man playing pinochle.

"She said who she was didn't she?" said the counterman. "Nathan Elbaum," he said, extending his hand. "I wanted to write when I was young."

"Yeah," cracked a guy at the pool table. "Numbers."

Natie Elbaum had squeezed enough blood from the narrow streets of Baltimore to buy and sell Trixie's family five times over, but to judge by his appearance and the hole-in-the-wall business his father started at the turn-of-the-century, you would have taken him for the junkman Trixie so badly sought.

"How can I help you, sweetheart?" he said.

"You own the houses on Cabbage Alley."

The daily lottery number was announced and the room groaned.

"Right around the corner," said Natie.

"All of it?"

"All that's left."

"I'm looking for anybody who used to rent or buy from you over there."

"Why's 'at?" said a guy reading the *Racing Form*. "Historical society putting up markers where the whorehouses used to be?"

"I want the story before it's gone."

"Wait no more," said Natie, inviting Trixie behind the counter. He led her past the men, down a long hall jammed floor-to-ceiling with glass jugs of water capped with corks, and down to a dank, dark basement.

"You're still in business?" asked Trixie.

"Mostly we talk about people who are dead," said Natie. "And horses who run like they're dead."

Trixie stayed close behind Natie as they descended wobbly steps, the walls dry and cool, her hand, afraid of falling again.

They reached the bottom and she blurted out: "Did you know Orlo?"

"The junkman?"

Trixie's heart jumped and she stumbled.

"Watch yourself," said Natie, pulling a chain on a light.

"Did you?"

"My father did."

"And he is?"

"Dead," said Natie. "My old man knew everybody and everybody he knew is dead."

"What did he tell you about Orlo?"

"That he collected junk."

"And Leini?"

"Who?"

"Eleini Leftafkis. Married a man named Papageorgiou."

"Never heard of her. Try Greektown."

"I think they lived in one of your properties."

"Who didn't? Whose name was on the lease?"

"I don't know."

"Let's see what we've got here," said Natie, pulling the drawer of a file cabinet, running his fingers over crumbling folders. "My old man kept immaculate records."

Natie pulled a manila envelope bound with twine, blew dust off of it, handed it to Trixie, and kept digging.

Walking the package to the bare bulb on the ceiling, Trixie found records from the mid-1930s showing that a man named Saul Solomon Pincherele defaulted on a mortgage held by St. Casimir Savings Loan for 408 Cabbage Alley. A week later, Elbaum Properties bought the house at auction.

Folded into the lease was a yellowed newspaper article, dated 1927, that ran with a picture of a woman identified as Agnes Pincherele. The story had appeared in the *News American* without a byline. The caption said the woman was a sculptor and the photo showed her sitting beneath a Star of David in the backyard of 408 Cabbage Alley. An unidentified baby sat on her lap.

Records for 410 included a lease signed by Saul Pincherele, several years of on-time rent payments, and then a long break followed by eviction papers.

"Gee monetti!" said Natie, pulling a metal canister from the cabinet.

"What?"

"Film," said Natie, picking rotted tape from the sides of the can and holding a length of it up to the light bulb. "It's the Star. Me and my brother Moe in front of the Star."

"You took movies of peoples' houses after you threw them out?"

"We didn't take their houses, young lady. The banks did. My father, he liked gadgets. Anything new that came out, he had to have it."

Trixie looked at the rent the Pinchereles had paid before the Depression, multiplied it by five square miles of rowhouses, allowed for inflation, and multiplied that by a half-century plus twenty.

"You could have helped them instead of taking advantage of them."

"We tried to save the Star," said Natie. "So many tenants. Kids and drunks and bottles smashed against it. Jews from all over the city came to see it. Do you have any idea how many people lost their homes?"

"That was a once-in-a-lifetime house."

"Was it more important than other people's houses because there was art in the yard?"

"There was a room upstairs made of velvet," said Trixie.

"Says who?"

"Everybody knows it."

"I don't remember anything like that," said Natie. "The story was that the Catholic Polack made the Star for her Jewish husband as a wedding gift."

"What the fuck happened to the God of mercy?"

Natie liked this kid, liked her right off. He liked her mind and her moxie even though her haircut reminded him of the camps his relatives had not survived as his father was taking people's homes in America.

He handed her the film.

"I know how much it hurts to see things torn down."

"You do?"

"I want a favor."

"What?"

"When I was growing up, God was God and a Jew was a Jew and nobody pointed fingers."

Trixie's heart beat against the can of film.

"But today, a phenomenon!" said Natie. "Young Jews more religious than their parents, more strict than their great-grandparents in the *shtetl*. Right here in Baltimore families with eight, nine, ten, eleven kids. Making up for the six million. I want you to write about it."

"As payment for the film?"

"As a favor."

Back upstairs, heading out the door to find the baby in the

newspaper photo, Trixie asked Natie what he'd do with Cabbage Alley once all of the houses were gone.

"It sat for this long," he said. "It can sit some more."

As Baltimore's public works strike ground on, scavengers came to Cabbage Alley to take tin for the ceilings of gentrified rowhouses along the water and bricks for backyard patios and Natie Elbaum could not free his mind of the young woman who'd shamed him under his own roof.

When the daily number was announced, Natie thought of Trixie.

When he won or lost a hand of cards.

And especially when another sucker signed the dotted line or, on his way home at night, driving out of the city, he caught a glimpse of what was left of Cabbage Alley.

He saw Trixie's face and heard her voice.

"Taking people's homes was merciful?"

Very early one morning—walking out the back of the building together after a night shift in which a man had clubbed a loved one into a coma over the rights to a bacon cheeseburger—Trixie sat Alvarez down on the curb of Guilford Avenue.

A gibbous moon hung over the dome of Johns Hopkins Hospital like a pulsing sack of blood and trucks pulled away from the loading docks with 238,000 copies of the morning paper, one more edition of *The Sun* without a Trixie Loo byline on anything that mattered.

Trixie touched her knee to Alvarez's and asked where she could find a projector to screen vintage movies.

"For what?" said the night editor, anxious to get home to his kitchen table.

"For this," said Trixie, pulling the film from her backpack.

"Take it to the Pratt."

"The hospital?"

"The library," said Alvarez, fingering a pair of miniatures in his pocket, enough to last the short walk home. "I have to go."

Alvarez stood up and Trixie pulled out a flask of good liquor.

"Wait a minute," she said and took a sip and held the flask out to him.

Alvarez looked at Trixie, looked at the flask, looked around, looked at Trixie again, and sat down. He took a long swig and then another.

"The audio-visual room at the Pratt has anything you need," he said. "Tell 'em you're a friend of mine."

They passed the flask back and forth; Trixie barely wetting her lips with the booze, trying to flirt with Alvarez as the good liquor worked on his childishness and his grandiosity, but not his libido.

"You know what you need, Trix?"

"What?"

"A private audience."

"Tonight?"

Alvarez drained the flask and held it up to the moon above the tin pyramid that topped the Maryland Penitentiary across the Jones Falls.

"An audience," he said, standing. "With our Kerouac, our Wolfe, our Whitman!"

Trixie laughed and Alvarez began reciting prose carved upon his heart.

"The way the late afternoon sun falls against the Formstone facade of Queenie's Confectionery on Belnord Avenue...that dull orange light and cracks in the sidewalk choked with emerald weeds...that's where my yearning is..."

Trixie stared at Alvarez against the tea-colored moon.

"Did you write that?"

"A leprechaun did," said Alvarez, handing back the empty flask. "Our Kerouac. Our Whitman."

Trixie stored the Elbaum film in her refrigerator and showed up at the all-night waterfront diner for her audience with Baltimore's Leprechaun of Letters.

She studied stained photo copies of the legend's manuscripts that Alvarez had given her and made notes in a composition book covered with purple velvet, whispering the cadence of the narrative.

At the top of a blank page she wrote: "June 20, 1999."

Below that: "The Legend of the Velvet Room."

"...like water from the sacred font...a language lost in well-washed sheets...pulling her fast and urgent from her velvet shroud...filling her until she laughs...movies across the faces of rowhouses that deny, through screened teeth: 'What matters is to know this tale...'"

As Trixie measured the lines with the tip of her pen, her appointment bounced into the diner; a man who'd hack-sawed copy for *The Sun* before Loo was born, had mentored three generations of aspiring writers for minimum wage at community colleges, ghosted memoirs for manufacturing tycoons, and filed marquee tragedies for tabloids before dropping out of the world to sit alone at the K-Mart Cafe and scribble fiction on the back of index cards.

He slapped hands with the man at the grill—"Hey Hoss!"—whispered something that made the man laugh and sat across from Trixie beneath a neon sign that glowed: "Sip & Bite."

"Miss Loo?"

"Tom Nugent?"

"At your service."

Behind Trixie's head hung a lacquered essay about the diner that Alvarez had written for the paper back before they'd parked him on the night desk.

Nugent pointed to it and said: "He thinks an awful lot of you."

Trixie, who'd been in Baltimore nearly six weeks without eating a crab, stood to read it as Lefty the Greek came out from behind the grill with menus. Though gossip held that pig's feet had fueled Orlo and Leini's lust, the clown swore they liked crab cakes best. Trixie ordered a crab cake platter.

"Soft crab on white toast," said Nugent. "And a Greek salad."

Lefty nodded, took the menus, and pointed to the Alvarez article on the wall.

"How is our friend?" the cook asked.

"Not so good," said Nugent and Lefty turned away to make their meal.

"What do you mean not so good?" asked Trixie.

"Not so good."

"How long have you known Rafael?"

"Twenty years."

"How did you meet?"

"I'd just quit *The Sun* and was hitch-hiking to New Orleans to drink myself to death," said Nugent. "Threw my wallet in a trash can on Hanover Street and stuck my thumb out. Alvarez was in the neighborhood working a murder. Back when fourteen-year-olds killing each other was still news. He picked me up, bought me a drink, and talked me out of it. We spent the rest of the day looking for my wallet. That's the day I got sober."

"How?"

"I don't exactly know," said Nugent. "But it helped to stop drinking."

"Why can't Rafael get sober?"

"Because he won't stop drinking."

Lefty brought the food to the table with two large cups of iced-tea. He stood by the table until Trixie assured him that the crab cakes were delicious.

"What was Rafael like when he was my age?"

"He believed," said Nugent.

Tears welled as Trixie savored a forkful of golden crab; the veins in the whites of Nugent's eyes maroon and splintered, worse than the violet arcs coursing through Ruthie's ears and not as bad as the brown puddles in Alvarez's eyes.

"I'm throwing my life away here," she said.

"You will always love the city you die in," said Nugent, eating with gusto.

"The editors say a lot of things. All the right things. But all they really want is for us to catch important people with their pants down or their hands in the till. The summer is half over and I still don't have enough to write what I want."

"You'll never have enough."

"Never?"

"One day you just have to write it."

Nugent yanked a crispy flipper off of his crab, gobbled it, and leaned forward on his elbows.

"Keep making passes at it," he said. "Like water over a stone."

Commas, music, water, stones.

"Fuck it," said Trixie.

"Who's left?" asked Nugent. "Who's still alive?"

"The daughter."

"Find her."

"She won't talk to me."

"Try again."

"When?"

Nugent ordered a scoop of ice cream in a paper cup.

"Now," he said.

Trixie gathered up her notes, Lefty refused to take her money, and out they went, down to the end of Clinton Street, Nugent standing by the water's edge with a half-cup of melted ice cream, gazing at the Salvage House shimmering in the moonlight, gargoyle pigs on every corner of the roof.

The writer slurped the dregs of the cup and complimented Trixie on her taste in narrative.

"Nobody can tell you what to write," he said. "All I know for sure is there's no way to tell a sincere story without telling your own."

"But how do you *make* somebody talk?"

"Unless you can trick them into it, there ain't no way."

Trixie sat alone in the auditorium of the Enoch Pratt Free Library on Cathedral Street, waiting in the dark for the show to begin. Cities may molt but there is nothing sadder than velvet worn to threads.

The brittle film began to roll. Trixie perspired. And paradise flickered across the screen.

Like God, the film was silent.

Like nature, it exposed itself without explanation.

Why did the clown know just enough to sell her one half-truth after another?

Where was the Pincherele baby?

How could Alvarez pay so much attention to her writing but not to her?

The film had been shot outdoors, the camera fixed on the Star of David nearly a century before weather and vandals and neglect had reduced it to chalk. Below the Star, fruit hung from trees and flowers rose from buckets. Ivy climbed from a bathtub filled with dirt. A fountain bubbled and Trixie watched a young Natie Elbaum—all ears and dark, piercing eyes—cut-up with his friends and family, the Star ablaze in the sun.

Stroking her arm, Trixie imagined herself in the garden and searched for clues, but the only thing the film confirmed was that Natie had been very handsome, his brother less so, and their father was good at making money and bad at making movies.

She cursed the family for not shooting film inside the house, for trading something priceless for a trickle of rent when something snapped and the screen went white, spools sputtering in the dark. The projectionist patched the film together and ran it down to Trixie.

"Have it transferred to video," he said. "Then you can make as many copies as you like."

Trixie thanked him.

Were reporters not salesmen?

You need to give people something for a taste of their grief.

"Leini didn't die young for Christ's sake," barked Ted after peeking at Trixie's sonnet when she got up to use the bathroom at one of the clown's haunts. "You can go up to Greektown right now and find a dozen moustached shrews who grew better roses than Leini did."

Trixie found Little Leini on the side of the Salvage House, mashing a seaweed concoction she sprayed on her peach trees to protect them from frost.

"I brought you something," said Trixie as Little Leini tried to stare her down.

"What?"

Trixie held up a video of the Elbaum film.

"Cabbage Alley from the old days. You have a VCR?"

Little Leini put down her churning stick, wiped her hands on her house dress, and walked inside with Trixie behind her. Taking the video from Trixie, she popped it into a VCR behind the counter and watched black-and-white ghosts flicker across a TV hanging from the ceiling on chains; her uneven eyes misting at sun-bleached images of a Star rotating through the ages.

Trixie stopped the tape.

"Want it?"

Little Leini glared at her.

"Then talk to me," said Trixie.

"No cameras," said Little Leini. "No tape recorders."

"Okay," said Trixie, putting the tape in her backpack.

"But it'll cost you," said Little Leini.

"The tape?"

"The tub."

"What tub?"

"Don't play dumb with me."

"Was there a velvet room?"

"Bring me the tub."

"But..."

"The tub."

From the moment Trixie Loo walked into his hole-in-the wall office on Eastern Avenue to ask questions no one could answer and make accusations no one could defend, Natie Elbaum prayed that the young reporter would come back.

He prayed and waited and conjured a shaved head that reminded him of slaughtered relatives. The sun passed from one side of street to the other and the money kept rolling in; Natie Elbaum vexed without relief in the month since Trixie Loo noted the injustices filed away in his basement.

Rushing in one afternoon when she should have been looking for the victims of a house fire on Binney Street, Trixie ran to the counter where Natie stood thinking of her and shouted: "I found someone!"

"A true detective!" laughed Natie.

"I have to go out of town."

"Now?"

"Tomorrow. After work."

"Send me a card."

"I need a favor," said Trixie.

"Name it."

"The tub from the velvet room."

"It'll be waiting for you when you get back."

"You mean it?"

"Now my favor," said Natie, walking Trixie to the door, out of earshot of the buzzards playing cards. Standing with her on the curb in the early evening, watching an A-rabber walk a pony cart of watermelons up Broadway, Natie stared into Trixie's unblinking eyes and she hoped he wouldn't press her to write about Orthodox Jews in Baltimore.

"Yes?"

"I want you to forgive me," said Natie.

"For what?"

"For the greed that ran in my life."

"How can...?"

"Just say you forgive me."

"I'm not religious," said Trixie.

"Neither am I."

"Why me?"

"Why not you?"

"I can do that for you, Mr. Elbaum."

"I wish there was velvet left to give you."

"There was velvet?"

"You believe there was velvet?"

"With all my heart."

"Then so do I."

"You've done so much," said Trixie.

"I wrote checks to 613 charities a year," said Natie. "I could have done a lot more."

The next day, with Trixie's ankle healed enough to put her full weight on it without wincing, the city split open.

A little before 6 p.m. on the Friday before the Fourth of July, as Trixie waited for her shift to end, inmates began tossing bodies from the roof of the Maryland Penitentiary around the corner from *The Sun*.

The police scanner jammed, sirens wailed without end, and phones rang off the hook. Black smoke and flames rose from the metal pyramid atop the prison and fires began consuming derelict rowhouses around the prison that the city hadn't gotten around to razing.

"Shit," said Trixie, watching from the newsroom windows, her plane set to leave in an hour, Natie's favor dancing before her eyes with the flames.

Peter Hermann, the paper's ace, ran the five blocks to the prison with six photographers and an acolyte intern in tow. He called the desk five minutes later to report five dead and off-the-record information that armed inmates were emptying cells.

Every reporter, editor, photographer, clerk, and copy boy was called in; secretaries ordered 100 pizzas and cases of soda. Arbitrari directed the coverage like Patton hitting Morocco and Alvarez straggled in with a hangover and a cheesesteak sub.

"Rafael," whispered Trixie. "I've got to get out of here."

Arbitrari barked at them: "Call the governor and find out when the goddamn National Guard is coming."

Correctional officers were dead, social workers were dead, ministers and visitors and many, many inmates dead and dying. Seven, eight, nine as the riot spread into the neighborhood around the prison; grocers dead, crossing guards dead, and children dead as the Monster that Ate Baltimore City fanned through the city.

Arbitrari caught Trixie edging toward the door.

"Where are you going?"

"I'm off," said Trixie.

Arbitrari turned away and made a bee-line for Alvarez, who looked worse than usual without the afternoon nap and pick-me-up that usually braced him for the night shift.

"My office," said Arbitrari, but before Alvarez could follow, the editor wheeled on him.

"Her project is spiked. Now sit your ass down and be a newspaperman for ten hours. This paper needs fairy tales like Baltimore needs more drug addicts."

"People love fairy tales," said Alvarez.

The veins in Arbitrari's head bulged and a corpuscle popped behind his left eye. Eleven dead, twelve dead, and then a jump to twenty-two; psychopaths running free in the falling night.

"I believe in a fucking velvet room like I believe that clock you couldn't stop writing about gave advice," Arbitrari screamed. "We're sending sportswriters to cover a massacre and she's going home?"

An inmate who'd scaled the metal pyramid fired a handgun at a police helicopter before a sharpshooter dropped him. Shock Trauma choppers rushed wounded over *The Sun* building, drowning out Arbitrari's tirade, but not so much that everybody else in the room didn't get the gist of it.

He moved close enough to Alvarez to kiss him and yelled: "You no longer have a drinking problem. You're a drunk. You want to end up like Yengich?"

"I've already lived longer than Nick."

Arbitrari felt his hands rising for Alvarez's throat.

"I'm telling you that she better get her head in the game and yours out of her drawers."

Clerks shouted: "Hermann on line six...! The governor on four...! A gas line in the 400 block of Preston Street just blew!"

"We're in business to print the truth," screamed Arbitrari, needing Alvarez to be at his best tonight and work hand-in-glove with a rewrite pro named Ettlin to shepherd thousands of inches of ragged notes into needlepoint. No time to teach the kids how it's done.

"Fuck your truth," said Alvarez, leaving Arbitrari to take dictation from a reporter who'd crawled beneath a police cruiser on the prison parking lot.

Twenty-three dead, twenty-four dead, thirty-one dead.

As media from around the world converged on Baltimore, Trixie slipped unnoticed from the newsroom.

Instead of packing her bag, she began throwing plates and saucers against the walls, the sink, the floor.

A waste, she sobbed, hurling crockery.

A failure.

I could have gone anywhere, she cried.

But I had to come here.

Dropping to the floor, shards cutting her knees, Trixie bled and wept and called out for a soon-to-be-gone-from-this-world great-grandmother who only cared if she was feeling well. Getting up, Trixie threw a change of clothes in her backpack and rushed to the airport.

Minnie Fischer would not die on her again.

An umber moon rose behind opaque clouds as Trixie's jet winged away from Baltimore and she imagined Orlo and Leini staring at the same tea-tinted disc, lying below the skylight in the velvet room.

She picked fresh scabs on her knees and solicited the dead lovers.

How much does it take?

To live as you please.

Trixie had amazed herself in the newsroom and wondered what the consequences might be.

She played with the word.

Consequence: neither positive nor negative.

It just is.

As the landing gear hit the runway, Nugent's voice spoke to Trixie in the squeal of the tires: "The story is *always* in front of you..."

After talking her way into an invalid's rowhouse on the periphery of the penitentiary, Nadine crept across a block of roofs, shimmied down a rain spout, and hid behind a corner grocery for a front row seat to the carnage.

Paralyzed before a scene she couldn't wait to write about—four Satans stripping a fat parson in front of a bonfire—Nadine dropped to her belly on the sidewalk and asked herself: "What would Trixie do?"

The nurse at the Shomrei Emunah old age home led Trixie down a long, tiled hallway, a mezuzah on every door, and asked if she was a relative.

"I've been here a long time," the nurse said. "And I can't remember Mr. Pincherele ever having a visitor."

"Our families go back," said Trixie as Sunday papers fat with riot news began landing on doorsteps across Maryland. "Back to Baltimore."

"He loves talking about Baltimore," said the nurse. "It's today he has trouble with."

"Good," said Trixie.

"Excuse me?"

"Nothing."

The nurse opened a door to a room at the end of the hall, walked in and said: "Sol? You have a visitor."

"Huh? What?"

"Uncle Sol," said Trixie, moving toward the bed as the nurse left the room, a black and white photo on the night table of Paul and Teddy in front of adjoining rowhouses across the street from a slaughterhouse.

Sol sat up.

"Hi," said Trixie.

"Who are you?"

"I'm a friend of Orlo and Leini."

"Oh."

"Do you know them?"

"Billy and Lenny?"

Trixie took a palm-sized tape-recorder from her pocket, hit the record button, and slipped it next to Sol's pillow.

"Can I take your picture?"

"How do I know you?"

"You don't," said Trixie. "When did you live on Cabbage Alley?"

"Where?"

"When did you live in Baltimore?"

"My mother was from Baltimore. I only lived there for a couple years. Then we had Depression."

"What do you remember?"

"About what?"

"What do you remember about your house in Baltimore?"

"A garden behind the house. Things my parents told me."

"What did you like best?"

"Got my first haircut under the Star."

"Do you have anything from the house?"

"My family's all dead."

Trixie picked up the picture from Sol's bedstand.

"Are these your parents?"

"Yes."

"Who took the picture?"

"The photographer."

"When did your parents die?"

"Dad drowned on the river during the war when a barge capsized.

Mom died a couple years ago."

"You're kidding."

"They lived long on her side."

"How old are you?"

"Seventy-three."

"What did they tell you about Baltimore?"

"It was sort of like a *shtetl*."

"A stencil?"

"*Shtetl*," said Sol, spitting phlegm into a plastic cup. "A Jewish village in Europe. They didn't die, but they don't exist."

"Like the velvet room?"

"Mama always said how happy we were in Baltimore. They were going to buy every house in the alley."

"Cabbage Alley?"

"Between Fleet and Eastern."

"Did your mother keep making art when you moved?"

"She cleaned other people's houses. White people in New Orleans never saw anybody clean like a Polack from East Baltimore."

"Did they ever talk to you about a room at the very top of your old house that belonged to the junkman?"

"Nobody is allowed up there."

"But did they talk about it?"

Sol groaned and leaned toward his nightstand. He opened the drawer and took out a stained metal key.

"This will get you in."

"You were inside?"

"Nobody is allowed up there."

Trixie jiggled the key in her palm and moved the warm metal across her lips.

"But you went up, right?"

Sol flinched.

"No Mama. Honest."

Trixie put the key in her pocket, pulled a tiny video recorder from her satchel, and hit the play button.

"Look," she said, holding the screen to Sol's milky eyes.

"Huh?"

"Right here," said Trixie.

Sol wet his pajamas.

"Oh my God."

"What do you remember?"

"A crown of feathers."

"What?"

"I didn't go up, mama."

"It's the backyard. Where you had your haircut."

"I swear, I didn't."

Bad guys were dead and good guys were dead in a long weekend of paybacks.

Some inmates were too crazed with resentments to run.

Little Melvin took a bullet alongside a retired *Afro-American* editor who visited the prison once a week to help the aging thug with his memoirs. Crowbar Carducci received an ice pick in his good eye from a black inmate who remembered getting beaten up every time he walked through Little Italy as a kid.

And the Monster that Ate Baltimore City could not keep the faces of his victims from smiling at him as a gang of Schroeder Street boys whittled his scrotum with sharpened spoons.

After a long, exhausting night of asking themselves what Trixie might do—admitting it to no one as the riot dimmed to embers—the interns began gathering at a waterfront after-hours bar to celebrate.

Giddy with accomplishment, they danced with the same abandon as the inmates had rampaged; primed with adrenaline to crow and screw and sweat and shower before returning to the story; honoring their baptism by fire by doing the Monster Mash atop a bloody pie.

Forty-six dead in the worst prison carnage in American history.

Uglier than New Mexico.

Bigger than Attica.

Every ten minutes, someone new showed up at the Good Love Bar with a source, a friend, a lover, and fresh details of the storm that had battered 954 Forrest Street and leveled two dozen city blocks around it.

Along with the rookies came veteran reporters invigorated by the buzz of a big story and the enthusiasm of the kids working it.

A buxom redhead who fancied herself the heir to Dorothy Parker's wit showed up with a cop she'd met at the riot, promising him anything if he told her everything.

Ettlin roused Jay Spry from his retirement bed to show the old rewrite man it could still be done right; Zorzi came with Roger Twigg in the back of an unmarked police cruiser; and David Simon made a cameo appearance with a weekend anchorwoman.

Even Arbitrari showed his face long enough to buy a round.

Only Alvarez—who'd stayed behind to proof the index to a special riot section—didn't post, walking home from the office to drink himself stupid, passing out while trying to jerk off to visions of Trixie.

"Hey, hey," roared the Fleshtones from the Good Love's loudspeakers. "Sha la la la."

The newsroom grooved together in a sweaty mass: drunk and delirous and self-important.

Dawn splintered across the waterfront, illuminating the harbor from luxury marinas to the dereliction of Cabbage Alley, casting knives toward the back of the only intern absent.

"Where's Loo?"

"Spread across the City Desk, being edited by Alvarez!"

"Where's Loo?"

"Kneeling in front of Alvarez, looking for commas!"

"Where's Loo-bop-a-lula?"

Someone ducked into the alley to blow a joint. A White House correspondent slipped out a side door with two secretaries from the editorial department. A guy from sports was throwing up in the bathroom, and three copy editors came to their senses and decided to walk to the corner for breakfast.

And the photo intern with a bad crush on Trixie—pressed into service from the James H. Jackson Memorial Lacrosse Tournament—was incredulous that she would pass up the story of the decade to chase a velvet goose.

Incredulous, impressed, and about to hurt someone if they didn't stop talking about her.

"Where's Alvarez?"

"Sucking vodka from Trixie's ass!"

"That broken-down motherfucker. I don't think he'd get off his ass to interview Christ nailed to the back of a flat-bed truck."

"That bald-headed fortune cookie thinks she's so fucking great. What's the big secret?"

The photo intern put his drink down, stood up, and decked the smart-ass with a right to the ear, jumping onto the kid as he fell, the dancing unimpeded around them. A bouncer tossed both of them onto the sidewalk and a second photographer raced out to shoot the brawl.

Before the cops showed up, fifty beepers went off at once.

The riot had flared.

"Where do you really think she is?" asked the hung-over interns, eating egg sandwiches and drinking coffee across from the Penitentiary with firefighters on stand-by.

Walking down Bourbon Street with a key around her neck to a room that didn't exist.

Flying back to Baltimore.

Watching the flames that had destroyed her career eat away at the Penitentiary roof.

On the far southeastern edge of the Holy Land, down along O'Donnell Street, are the cemeteries.

Protestant and Jewish, Greek Orthodox, and acres of Catholics.

First, Trixie found the right graveyard and then—in between a marker shaped like a Clipper ship, a bronze beer stein grafted to a stone marked "Wigmann," and a monument to five Chinese sailors who drowned in the Great Baltimore Hailstorm of 1917—a patch of grass and a peach tree.

A tree coaxed from a cutting taken behind the Salvage House.

Leini's son lay beneath military marble in Normandy; her husband's skeleton rattled at the bottom of the sea, her lover's ashes came and went with the tides on the Patapsco, and her own corpse slept beneath a tree heavy with fruit in a forgotten cemetery of Germans.

Reduced through folly and insubordination to a newsroom clerk, Trixie plucked a peach in the middle of the workday and ate in silence.

Anyone could build a room out of velvet.

But how much skill did it take to be Eleini Papageorgiou?

Traffic hummed on Interstate-95. Blueberry bushes, remnants of old farms, separated seven acres of the dead from an eroding neighborhood of rowhouses. Under the tree, Trixie questioned a woman who, by the time she was Loo's age, had spent a dozen years in a foreign country, had loved in secret for four, and endured marriage for three.

And a baby.

What, she asked, did *you* want to be?

The summer was winding down and Trixie's only on-the-record source for a waterfront room of velvet was an alcoholic clown who demanded a half-pint of brandy for every lie he told.

Trixie spit out the peach pit and tossed it into tall grass.

She asked: "Did you take all the secrets with you?"

And got as much of a response as she did at the side of Solomon Pincherele's bed.

By mid-August—the long, sticky month that Alvarez said made him *feel* like a writer when he sat in front of a fan drinking beer in his underwear—Trixie had been asked out by a business reporter; a municipal accountant she'd interviewed when the Department of Recreation went broke; and got at least one call a week from a handful of boys who'd liked her in college.

But in the two-and-a-half months she'd been in Crabtown, she had not been on a real date or had sex with anyone but herself; restless evenings when she took the edge off of her ambition with fantasies of lovers rolling across a velvet floor only to be roused by the fear of being infected by the Monster that Ate Baltimore City.

Alvarez doesn't care, she thought, trying to fall back asleep.

He wouldn't care if I charted every comma and semi-colon of his fucked-up life.

But the photo intern, who'd discovered that his ancestors and Trixie's hailed from the same part of China, persisted. When Loo decided he could be of use, she made a date.

"Meet me at the Good Love in an hour," she said. "Bring your camera."

Trixie arrived first and fortified herself with a few drinks. When the photographer showed up, he bought a round and then another.

"Help me do something tonight," she said.

"Sure."

He noticed that Trixie's backpack, usually stuffed, was flat.

"You have to trust me," she said.

"Name it."

They left the bar and drove to the end of Clinton Street. As Trixie walked along the edges of the Salvage House, the photographer began taking pictures of his crush roaming the grounds of a perfect make-out spot.

Moon and stars and harbor lights shining on an old, spooky house at the water's edge.

Trixie waved the photog over and led him to a door in the back.

"What?" he asked.

"Watch."

Trixie took a towel from her backpack, wrapped it around her fist, and smashed a pane of glass above the doorknob.

"What are you doing?"

Trixie opened the door from the inside.

"Jesus Christ," said the photographer, following her into a hive of shadows, wondering if he'd have sex in the midst of a burglary as clocks ticked from unseen mantles.

Trixie braved the upstairs first, palming two complete dinner settings along the way; the photographer taking hundreds of shots in the dark, following Loo's sharp features through his lens, room to room until a door closed behind them.

"Fuck," she said, her flashlight shining off a million doorknobs, the walls lined with funhouse mirrors. The photographer used his flash and the light ricocheted a million times: knobs of glass, brass, metal, stainless steel, ceramic, crystal, and polished wood multiplied in the undulating mirrors.

Trixie tried one knob after another without finding one connected to a door. They walked in circles, bumped into each other, and, forgetting for a moment that they were locked inside a house they'd broken into, laughed at their taffy faces in the mirrors.

When it stopped being funny, Trixie ordered the photog to stop taking pictures and help her find the way out.

Two floors above them, Little Leini felt thwarted desire in her dreams. She was nine years old again, the age her mother had been when she left Greece, and George had her staring down a bowl of oatmeal in the kitchen on Ponca Street.

Her mother off somewhere with Orlo.

Off with Orlo.

Off with Orlo.

Trixie finally turned the right knob as Little Leini woke up gagging, her nightclothes soaked in sweat. Laying absolutely still, she thought of Loo and what a pain-in-the-ass the reporter was as Trixie trained a flashlight on baseboards leading to the basement, wanting to kill the clown who'd sold her a worthless floor plan.

On the way down, the photographer spent another roll of film on Trixie's intense, quirky features, thin neck and bony shoulders; down to a large, cool basement of stone with a bank of oak file cabinets along the wall, shelves dusty with dried seed and cobwebs.

He was convinced that Loo was headed for an unknown greatness. When it found her, he would have images to provide the world.

Rifling the file cabinets, Trixie found a drawer of Dinky Dolls still in their boxes and in her lust for things that did not belong to her, thought of Natie's request for absolution. She stuffed her bag with armfuls of papers and they left through the basement door.

Driving back downtown, the photographer asked Trixie if she wanted to get coffee.

"No thank you."

"A movie or something next week?"

"I don't think so."

"Well what was this?"

"An assignment."

The next day, Trixie placed a special order with Schlegel's at the Broadway Market, set the meat in a deep dish to marinate, and dropped in on Natie Elbaum to strike a deal.

"Everything is coming together," she told herself, calling the City Desk to say she wasn't feeling well, staying home to cook and clean and anticipate her interview with the only heir to the legacy of Orlo and Leini.

Bad idea, thought Alvarez, selecting two bottles of wine at the grocery store around the corner from his house, debating as he paid for it whether he would drink too much, a debate he hadn't won in twenty years.

I'll stay sober until I get home, he told himself, walking toward Trixie's apartment as she soaked a dozen fresh figs from Cabbage Alley in warm white wine. She mixed the ripe, violet fruit with crumbs of blue cheese and chopped rosemary to complement an entree she'd spent two days preparing.

Trixie lived in an efficiency atop the Peabody Book Shop and Beer Stube and the meal was almost ready when Alvarez ducked in for a quick one.

A kid from the Baltimore School for the Arts played ragtime on an upright piano in the corner, the music climaxing as a sleight-of-hand artist with a silver beard took the small stage, a vaudeville violinist named Dantini who looked like Noah and performed in a tuxedo and tennis shoes.

Alvarez had interviewed Dantini a thousand times in his reporting days and was a little surprised that the sorcerer was still alive.

The Stube, a Danube coffeehouse in the 900 block of North Charles Street, was opened by an Austrian seaman who'd landed in Baltimore about the time Orlo first asked Leini to go for a ride. Fitzgerald drank there when Zelda was getting her head shrunk at Hopkins. John Mason Rudolph wrote the bulk of his first blockbuster novel at a booth in the back. Alfred Kazin always stopped in for a sherry when he was in Baltimore to have his typewriter overhauled.

The only thing Alvarez had penned at the Stube was middle-aged juvenilia and his name on credit card slips.

As Dantini made a pair of dentures fly from the mouth of a woman near the stage, Trixie spooned grease from a broth of tomato and basil, conjuring the essence of assignation. She wrapped a half-dozen of the figs in basil leaves and thin slices of ham, slipped them under the broiler, and told herself it was a date.

Trixie had never been in love, not as far as she knew.

Not in the third grade and not at Yale.

She walked a plate of sliced oranges into the front room—the clown had told her that a peeled orange was Orlo and Leini's favorite treat—and set the fruit on a table draped with white cloth.

Sucking a crescent of orange, Trixie lit the candles, arranged photos of Orlo and Leini on the table, and knew she would sleep with her guest on the slightest overture.

Downstairs, Alvarez toasted Dantini farewell and made his way to Trixie's door.

"Hey," he said, holding out the bottles of wine.

"Hello."

Alvarez followed Trixie into the kitchen.

"What are we having?"

"Go sit," said Trixie.

"Do you have a corkscrew?"

"I'll bring it."

Alvarez went to the large front room—Trixie's parlor, study, and bedroom, her bed in front of a large picture window that looked on the first monument to George Washington in the United States.

He set the wine on the dinner table and began inspecting the books on her shelves: *All the President's Men*, Mencken's *Newspaper Days, Homicide: A Year on the Street*, and *Best Newspaper Stories* from 1990 to the present.

Alvarez stared beyond the gabled roofs toward his apartment, a windowless, basement hovel choked with old newspapers and empty bottles. On the table, he saw the pictures that Trixie had stolen.

One was a formal studio shot, not quite a wedding portrait.

Another showed Orlo and Leini on the deck of a Pratt Street watermelon barge.

A third, cracked and brown, was taken at the Salvage House stables and pictured Leini on the back of the junkman's favorite horse, a dray named Diz.

At the edge of the table, a toy monkey hung from a pole, drinking beer from a tiny can with a key between his teeth.

Alvarez wondered where Trixie was with the corkscrew when she appeared with the figs arranged atop a bowl of rice and a large tureen.

"Voila!"

She bid Alvarez to sit and ladled the entree into his bowl.

"Pig's feet," said Alvarez, poking the large, fatty knuckles with his fork.

"The way they ate it."

"How do you know?" he said, reaching for the corkscrew.

"I'm a reporter," smiled Trixie.

Alvarez uncorked the wine and ate politely, nodding toward the portrait of Orlo and Leini in a drugstore frame.

"I'm going to scan them into my laptop and mail them back," said Trixie.

"Reporters never return photos," said Alvarez, chewing slowly. He drained his glass, filled it again, and ate a slice of orange to keep from choking.

Trixie tried to swallow, gave up, and dropped her fork. She'd followed every faded jot and squiggle of the recipe scrawled in Orlo's hand across the back of a Ralph's Lunch menu.

Alvarez forced a few more bites and pushed his plate away, handing Trixie a fresh napkin to dry her eyes.

"I did everything, just like it said."

All day Friday cleaning the feet and soaking them in cold water; stewing the trotters tender before laying them between layers of clove, bay leaf, and pepper pods in a stone crock; rubbing the joints with salt, cracked black pepper, and a kiss of cayenne before pouring boiling cider vinegar into the crock and setting it to cool on a sill that faced George Washington.

"Stories are always better than facts," said Alvarez, wondering if Trixie was going to drink the rest of her wine. "I'd bet even Orlo and Leini enjoyed telling their story more than living it."

"Then tell me this," said Trixie, composing herself. "How come someone with your experience is stuck on the night desk?"

"You kids think it's so hard to break into this business," said Alvarez. "Let me tell you, it's a lot harder to get out."

"How so?"

"Hemingway said the only thing newspaper work was good for was learning to write a clean sentence," said Alvarez. "And then you'd better get out before you wind up middle aged and unskilled or it kills you. When I was your age, internships were for med students and every young reporter wanted to write the great American novel."

"Does your novel have a name?"

"Of course."

"What is it?"

"Oh sweetheart," said Alvarez, filling his glass. "I'm so sick of telling people the name of my unwritten novel."

"Come on," said Trixie. "Tell me over here."

Alvarez took the wine and followed her to the bed. They put pillows under their heads and took off their shoes.

"They're nominating Nadine's story of the barbecued chaplain for a Pulitzer," said Alvarez.

"We're not talking about my failure," said Trixie.

"I didn't want to go to college, all I wanted to do was write," said Alvarez. "But my parents enrolled me at Loyola while I rode around getting high and listening to the Who."

"What?"

"Who."

"Who?"

"The Who," said Alvarez. "Tommy."

"Hilfiger?"

"Never mind," said Alvarez, staring beyond the bottle to stars shining in the window, thinking about Keith Moon and how he'd overdosed on pills prescribed to curb his alcoholism, his face becoming more pinched with each swig of wine.

"After I graduated from Transfiguration High I made a deal with my father."

"Is he still living?"

"He was a tugboat man. And he could hold his liquor like a man," said Alvarez. "Told him if he'd get me a summer job on a ship I'd start college in the Fall. Fuck Hemingway. I was gonna be Melville."

"What happened?"

"Dad kept his end of the deal."

"What was your job on the boat?"

"Chipping paint and mopping floors. I'd get high and borrow the steward's typewriter to write fiction. Mostly I scribbled notes to girls. Every ten or eleven days we'd dock in New Orleans or Texas and they'd pay us off in cash. We'd hit Beaumont and I'd try to interview Johnny Winter's fifth grade teacher. On our last stop in New Orleans I rented a room above a grocery store. Wrote my parents to say I wasn't coming home."

"What did you write there?"

"Nothing that mattered," said Alvarez, his stomach rumbling; clove and mace working on the alcohol. "I smoked a lot of reefer and interviewed a generation of bluesmen before they passed. Almost got myself killed a few times. Kept thinking I'd write a book about the blues, but when Guralnick started publishing, I gave up. Took a clerk's job in the sports department of the local paper."

"*Times-Picayune*."

"Yep. Learned to write a tight game story, started drinking with the sportswriters and before I knew it, the way they talked was leaching into my prose."

"When did you come back to Baltimore?"

"When a job covering the city opened up on the *News American*."

"What's that?"

"An afternoon daily that everybody in East Baltimore read. It folded in '86."

"And you joined *The Sun*?"

"Uh-huh," said Alvarez, killing the first bottle of wine and letting it roll under the bed before getting the other one from the table. "They hired me because I knew where Canton ended and Highlandtown began."

"But you don't write anymore?"

"No," he said, laying next to her. "I lived all my stories."

"What's the best one you never wrote?"

Alvarez took a long swig and coughed onto his white shirt.

"The morning I woke up and thought I was Anne."

"Anne?"

"Anne Frank."

"Come on."

"And the bastards wouldn't let me write it."

"I wonder why."

"You think corporate journalism is afraid to take on the high rollers? Paterakis and Hackerman?" Alvarez tapped the wine stain on his breast. "They're more afraid of what goes on in here," he said.

"Tell me."

"It started with diarrhea and a fever. I was in the bathroom when she appeared beneath the skylight, just bones and eyes under a dirty blanket."

Trixie moved to cradle Alvarez.

"It was her but it was me," he said. "I mean, I was still me, but I was her. Fuck. I don't know. I was her and I was in love with her at the same time."

"How long did it last?"

"Not long enough."

Alvarez offered the wine to Trixie, who waved it off. He took two long gulps; wine on clove on vinegar on figs on cartilage of swine.

"I'd written ten thousand newspaper stories by then," he said. "Van Gogh descriptions of every weather pattern known to man. But I wasn't a writer."

"Why didn't you write about Anne?"

"I tried," said Alvarez, finishing the second bottle. "I took it to the editor I thought would be most sympathetic."

"Arbitrari?"

"Get real. It was a new editor, a woman who had a rep for being sensitive. She used to stop me in the hall to say how much she wanted to work with me. She wouldn't touch Anne."

"Who?"

"Nobody. She left to flack for a non-profit that teaches kids to write."

"What did you do?"

"Spent a month wondering if Anne would come back before pitching the story to a dozen other editors. It became the joke of the newsroom. That's when I..."

"Gave up?"

"Became an editor," said Alvarez, leaping from the bed for the toilet and breaking the picture window with his face, vomit and glass falling three stories to the sidewalk below, resting his sliced forehead on the windowsill as Trixie screamed, a warm breeze drying the blood on his face.

Maybe, he thought, I should just follow the puke down to Charles Street.

Bombarded all summer by lobbyists for the truth, Trixie sat him down on the edge of the bed, wiped his face with a warm towel, and settled the debate in her head: Anne was simply a spirit who'd appeared to Alvarez one-quart bottle at a time.

With the calm and dexterity of her father, Trixie walked Alvarez to the bathroom, sat him on the toilet, and began picking shards of glass from his face with eyebrow tweezers.

"I don't think anybody stopped you," she said, bandaging the cuts. "Everything turned out the way it did because you drink too much."

"A rabbi believed me. A Park Heights sage, a survivor who said I should have come to see him. He told me to let the angels fly and find my *bashert* on Earth."

"Booze is your *bashert*," said Trixie.

"No honey," mumbled Alvarez, squeezing the bones in her shoulder as he stood up. "No it's not."

Trixie helped him to the door where they argued about calling a cab. She made sure he held the rail on the way down and stood in the breeze blowing through her busted window to watch Rafael Alvarez stumble home below the spires.

The dishes from Trixie's pig's feet fiasco lay dirty in the sink all day Sunday as she laid in bed wondering what to do next.

The *Boston Globe* was set to hire twenty short-term interns for every department in the building.

The jobs came without benefits and the union was fighting it.

Like a snouted Buddha, the gargoyle pig sat on the City Desk all summer, staring at Alvarez without blinking until he began talking to it.

"How much time do I have left?"

"Did Orlo and Leini really exist?"

"Do I?"

One evening, the pig began to answer.

Walking into the newsroom to check the final edits on a nine-part series about race relations at the end of the twentieth century, Arbitrari found Alvarez trying to nurse the pig and gently led the night editor out of the building.

Little Leini had twice told Trixie to hit the road, the only surviving source to the Ballad of Orlo and Leini refusing to give her the time of day.

Until Trixie called the bitch's bluff in the last week of summer.

A pick-up truck with Natie Elbaum's seventy-year-old yard boy at the wheel lumbered to the end of Clinton Street, bounding over potholes with Orlo and Leini's honeymoon tub in the back. Trixie sat next to the driver with a fresh notebook.

"The house this tub came from," said Trixie. "you ever hear of a room there made of velvet?"

"No ma'am," said the driver, turning into a dirt lane that led to the Salvage House.

Trixie found Little Leini in the peach grove, sitting for her portrait in the late afternoon sun.

The house looked different to Trixie from the morning she waited for the sun to rise over the roof; different from the afternoon she'd stared at it from the bow of a tugboat; different from the night she'd broken in.

Different because today she'd make it talk.

Little Leini squinted at Trixie as she approached; the artist at the easel struggling, as Loo had struggled, to capture the last living link to the greatest clandestine love affair the world has ever known.

Natie's boy began unloading the tub and the artist set down his brushes to help. They set the tub on the side of the house and the driver asked Trixie if he should wait.

Trixie thanked him with $20 and said no.

The artist resumed painting, making another pass at the distance between his subject's eyes.

"I'm busy now," said Little Leini.

"Now," said Trixie, and the artist began packing up his equipment.

In a stand of weeds obscuring the chainlink fence separating the

Salvage House from the gas tanks of Standard Oil lay the photo intern. He'd bicycled down to help Trixie defy the shitbird with the bad eyes; shooting roll after roll of black and white film with a telephoto lens as Little Leini told Loo she'd only talk if nothing were printed in her lifetime.

Trixie pointed to the tub and promised nothing.

"How did you come to own this place?" she asked.

"Why do you care?"

"Because it's my story," said Trixie.

"That's where you're wrong, missie," said Little Leini, moving toward the house. "How'd you get the tub from the Jew?"

"I'll ask the questions," said Trixie, following Little Leini into the kitchen and opening her notebook.

Little Leini put a glass of tap water in front of Trixie and lit a cigarette. "So ask."

"What's your full, legal name?"

"Helen Leftafkis Pound."

"When were you born?"

"February 8, 1949."

"Where?"

"City Hospital."

"Where did you go to high school?"

"Patterson. Class of '67."

"Were you a hippie?"

"Right."

"College?"

"No."

"Married?"

"Never."

"How old were you when you realized the junkman was your mother's lover?"

"I knew before I was born."

"Come on."

"That's an old one, honey."

"Tell me about her."

"My mother came to this country when she was nine and was raised by a Greek couple across the street."

"Is it true she went back to Greece before you were born?"

"My mother never made it back. Depression got her."

"Your mother suffered from depression?"

"The Depression. Look it up. I had a brother killed in the war. I was born four years later."

"What was his name?"

"Jimmy.

"Jimmy what?"

"Papageorgiou."

"You go by Pound."

"I do."

"Why?"

"It's my name."

"Who was your mother's best friend?"

"Miss Francie. That boy who was painting my picture is her grandson. You ought to write about him instead of me. He's going to be famous."

"Miss Francie what?"

"Francesca Bombacci Boullosa."

"Where can I find her?"

"She's dead."

"Who's left alive who knew Orlo."

"Plenty."

"I haven't found anybody."

"Work your way up and down Broadway."

"How come Orlo and your mother never married?"

"They were."

"Where can I look it up?"

"They were married more than married people are married."

"How hard was it for them?"

"It was terrible."

"Any notebooks or diaries?"

"They lived their lives. They didn't waste time writing about it."

"What will you do with the tub?"

"Keep it."

"Who's Ted the Clown?"

"An asshole."

"Did he know your mother when she lived on Cabbage Alley?"

"My mother never lived on Cabbage Alley."

"Someone said there are Works Progress Administration folk songs about Orlo and Leini."

"Why don't you interview someone if they know so much."

This story is beneath her, thought Trixie.

Buried under the bricks.

I ought to ask the screen door who came and who went.

Who slammed.

And who got locked out.

Make the dead sit for their portrait.

"I'm asking you," said Trixie.

"I grew up with it," said Little Leini. "I ate breakfast, lunch, and dinner with it every day of my life."

"Pig's feet?"

"I never ate pig's feet with my mother."

Trixie threw her pen down.

"This sucks."

"It's what you came for."

Little Leini left the room and Trixie followed her through a hallway of china closets stuffed with enough Beatles memorabilia to send five kids to Yale—a hall that ended in a big front room where Little Leini could watch the harbor and do business at the same time.

"All of this used to belong to someone who thought they wanted it," she said. "But people get tired of what they have."

"Why have you been so hard on me?" asked Trixie.

"Because I'm not tired of what I have."

Trixie moved to a wall of antique typewriters.

"Do you still have your mother's typewriter?"

"Which one?"

"Mark Twain's typewriter."

"Oh yeah," said Little Leini. "That one over there. I think he wrote *Puddin'head Wilson* on it."

Trixie stood in front of it.

"May I?"

"Knock yourself out."

Trixie rolled a piece of paper into the carriage and began typing.

"She'll die young and leave this kettlecloth world of stain..."

Crumpling the paper, Trixie offered Little Leini $40 for it.

"Sold."

"Just tell me," said Trixie. "Did Orlo and Leini live in a room made out of velvet?"

"Sweetheart, once the speculators came, my father wasn't even allowed to go back in for his hat."

"Your father?"

"Yes."

"What are you saying?"

"I'm saying I've answered enough of your questions. I'm saying that if you don't return what you broke in and stole from me I'll have you locked up."

"It was awful," confessed Trixie.

"It always is," said Little Leini.

As Trixie lugged the typewriter up Clinton Street, dust and grime sticking to the sweat on her face, the photo intern appeared to carry the typewriter for her.

"How did you know I was here?"

"The clown told me."

Trixie shook her head.

"I got some good shots. In the yard and through the front window."

"Give me the film."

"Go out with me."

"I can't."

"That's too bad," said the photog, going his own way.

Three months had passed since Trixie watched Ruthie's balloon sail through the clouds above Patterson Park.

In that time, Ruthie had found herself with child in a bowed-to-broken neighborhood where people repaired motorcycles in their living rooms; Ted the Clown had moved on to the next sucker; Trixie's hair had grown long enough to run a comb through; and Alvarez had hit enough jackpots to be on permanent leave from the newsroom.

Trixie used her last hours in Baltimore to say goodbye.

Pulling away from the paper in her beat-up station wagon, she headed north on the Jones Falls Expressway with Van Morrison singing on the radio.

"It's the youth of a thousand summers..."

North past the scorched pyramid above the Maryland Penitentiary.

North with a bag of peanut butter and jelly sandwiches and an orange crate stuffed with stolen photos and velvet files.

North past the exit to Interstate-70 that would take her home as the Great Bolewicki Depression Clock tolled throughout the Holy Land.

"It's not too late, it's only the last summer day of the twentieth century..."

Trixie pulled off the highway, drove through a stone gatehouse, and onto a lane of oak trees rolling through a lush campus.

She found Alvarez beneath a tree with a reporter's notebook, doodling pictures of birds.

He smiled as her car approached, the sun going down beyond the treetops; his smile widening to a grin when she slipped out of her sandals—the air calm, the evening gorgeous—and sat down in front of him.

"Hi," she said, setting a large, awkward package wrapped in black plastic against the tree.

"Hey."

"You look good."

"Ought to," said Alvarez. "Haven't had a drink in seventeen days."

"How's Anne?"

"We're okay," said Alvarez. "You want a good story?"

"Always."

"They got your night editor locked up in the spin bin."

"The squirrel cage?"

"The funny farm," said Alvarez.

"It's very peaceful," said Trixie.

"I like your hair."

(Once Trixie arrived at her place of perfect waiting, her hair would grow down the middle of her back, a black, braided curtain rustling the dimple of her ass.)

"Thanks," said Trixie, handing Alvarez a sandwich and a plastic bottle of water. He cracked the seal and took a long swig.

"Ahh," he said. "I love to drink from the bottle."

"How are you making out with that?"

"Good. Scared, but good. They said we had to be honest if we were going to make it."

"That's the rule?"

"Accepted wisdom. We're only as sick as our secrets."

"Really?"

"Yeah."

"Okay," said Trixie. "Do you love me?"

In the ensuing silence, Alvarez heard a tinkling of bells like the ones announcing the consecration of the Eucharist at Mass, bells from an ice cream truck. The sound, riding a hint of the coming Fall, reminded him of school and how happy ice cream had made him when he was a young.

"Yes," he said. "I love you."

"Good," said Trixie, tearing the plastic from the object she'd propped up against the tree to reveal a Star of David made from broken china. "I made this for you."

(I might be Anne, but I'm not Jewish, thought Alvarez. Neither reporter nor writer. I ain't drunk, but I ain't sober.)

"What is it?"

"The Summer of Ninety-Nine," said Trixie. "It represents everything you taught me."

"What's that?"

"If I say something is real, it's real."

"Great," said Alvarez, glimpsing a group of his dorm-mates strolling the grounds in blue smocks and paper shoes. "I taught you the thing that got me here."

"Guess what my final story was?"

"Let's see," said Alvarez. "What holiday is it?"

"Labor Day."

"You interviewed union bosses on the state of organized labor?"

"No."

"Spent the afternoon at swimming pools asking kids if they were ready for school to start."

"Nope."

"Went to a mall to cover the end-of-summer clearance sales."

"Uh-uh."

"I give up."

"I walked around Baltimore asking people how they spent their summer."

"And?"

"They gave Nadine the job."

"Good for her."

"She worked hard," said Trixie.

"And everybody else?"

"To the winds."

"And the next school board meeting," said Alvarez, savoring the texture of the peanut butter, the sweetness of the jelly. "What are you going to do?"

Trixie turned the Star over and read verses she'd lettered across the back.

"...she'll die young and leave her beauty, yearning for the way beneath pressing eyes...this kettlecloth world of stain and detergent...a clatter of cutlery and bones to pick until the miracle lifts her skirt, a balm on her soap-washed skin and a junkman's hand to heal, pulling her from a shroud, giving life until she laughs out loud...a swirling skirt of velvet stars...smiles and sun and wage of sin: small deaths and hair undone..."

It was the most beautiful thing Alvarez had heard since "Don't Worry Baby" came on the radio in 1964.

He rubbed his eyes, wiped his nose, and spit.

"What's it called?"

"'The Legend of the Velvet Room.'"

The ice cream truck stopped in front of them and Alvarez fished a few dollars from his pocket.

"I'll get dessert," he said.

"Give me a Good Humor," said Trixie.

"Make it two," Alvarez told the man.

They began to walk, licking melted ice cream from the corner of their mouths, wiping each other's chins.

"I'm praying that I'll want to write more than I want to drink," said Alvarez.

After circling the the campus, they arrived at Trixie's car.

"They settled the public works strike today," said Trixie. "You know what that means?"

"What?"

"Goodbye Cabbage Alley."

"I tried to help you," said Alvarez.

"I know you did."

Alvarez kissed Trixie's lips and she drove toward the setting sun to live with her great-grandmother on Duncombe Street, determined to get as much of the story as she could; back to a tiny bedroom in Chinatown where she took naps on a velvet sofa and read books on the floor; the French doors from the velvet room—a farewell gift from Natie Elbaum—strapped to the roof of her wagon, Mark Twain's typewriter under a pile of dirty laundry.

Hurtling back to the last place she remembered being happy.

Alvarez stood at the gatehouse until the car was a speck on the horizon, biting his ice cream stick in half as the Leprechaun whispered through the trees: "That's where my yearning is..."

Born in 1958, Rafael Alvarez is a lifelong Baltimorean. He is the author of *The Fountain of Highlandtown* and *Hometown Boy*. He can be reached at rafaelalvarez@sevarez.com.

Contributors

Jim Burger, a freelance photographer, was born in Uniontown, Pennsylvania, in 1960, the year Bill Mazerowski of the Pittsburgh Pirates hit the homerun that defeated the New York Yankees in the World Series. He moved to Baltimore in 1978 to attend the Maryland Institute, College of Art, graduating in 1982. Burger lives in Baltimore.

Jonathon Scott Fuqua painted the Salvage House that appears on the book's cover. He has published three books, including the novel *The Reappearance of Sam Webber*. Fuqua is Writer in residence at the Carver Center for the Arts in Baltimore County and teaches fiction, drawing, and watercolor in Baltimore.

Jade Gorman made the crockery mosaic of the Star of David (pictured in "The Legend of the Velvet Room"). A writer and researcher based in Baltimore, Gorman holds a master's degree in English from the University of Maryland.

Jenny Keith wrote Trixie's poem, "The Legend of the Velvet Room." She grew up in Virginia and moved to Baltimore in 1983. Keith has published her poetry in local journals.

Elizabeth Malby was born in Cleveland, Ohio, in 1970. She graduated with a degree in photojournalism from Kent State University in 1993. Malby is known for her portraits. A resident of Baltimore's Bolton Hill neighborhood, she has been a staff photographer at the *Baltimore Sun* since 1998.

Acknowledgments

I would like to thank Gloria Alvarez, Maryann Zen Fiebach, Kerry Ann Oberdalhoff, John Rivera, Joseph Truong, Norman Wilson, Andria Yu, and Bill Zorzi, Jr. for their work with this manuscript.